The Nexus Guardian

Tony Coco

Published by Tony Coco, 2024.

THE NEXUS GUARDIAN

First edition. October 10, 2024.

Copyright © 2024 Tony Coco.

ISBN: 979-8227115201

Written by Tony Coco.

Table of Contents

The Nexus Guardian

What if the ordinary was just a veil for the extraordinary?

Vivian, a restless 12-year-old boy bored with the monotony of school and life, has always felt there was something more out there, something beyond the everyday routines that define his world. When he volunteers for a strange science experiment involving an unfinished time machine, he suddenly finds himself swept into a mysterious dimension—a place where the rules of reality no longer apply.

Welcome to the Nexus, the heart of the multiverse, a realm where infinite worlds intersect and where chaos and balance hang by a thread. Guided by the brilliant yet enigmatic Professor Arcturus, Vivian soon discovers that his journey isn't just about escaping his life—it's about saving countless others.

But as the Nexus faces the growing threat of dark rifts and a powerful figure determined to unleash chaos, Vivian must come to terms with a power he never knew he had: the Quantum Spark, an ancient artifact capable of shaping reality itself.

Faced with impossible choices, shifting dimensions, and battles against forces older than time, Vivian must rise to become a protector of the multiverse. The fate of all realities depends on him, but how do you fight something that cannot be contained?

"The Nexus Guardian" is an epic fantasy adventure filled with mind-bending science, magical realms, and a coming-of-age tale where one boy's quest for purpose leads him to become the last defense against the unraveling of the multiverse.

Chapter 1: The Boredom of Existence

The soft hum of the anti-gravity hover-boards filled the air, gliding seamlessly above the city streets as Vivian stared out of the classroom window. Beyond the school's glass dome, towering skyscrapers blinked with holographic advertisements that promised new gadgets and dazzling distractions, but none of it stirred a flicker of interest in him. The future had arrived in all its glory, yet to Vivian, it felt devoid of wonder.

At twelve years old, he had already grown tired of everything. It wasn't that he didn't like life, but it all seemed...pointless. Home was the same thing every day: his parents talking about work, a silent dinner, and hours spent in his room, scrolling through endless feeds of mind-numbing entertainment. School wasn't any better. It was all predictable, robotic almost. Wake up, go to class, sit through lectures, and go home. Repeat. There was no mystery, no adventure—nothing to ignite his curiosity anymore.

And curiosity had once been Vivian's defining trait.

He remembered how he used to get excited about learning things—how the world seemed so big, filled with endless possibilities. But somewhere along the way, he had lost that spark. Now, it was all just routine.

"Vivian?" The teacher's voice jolted him from his thoughts. "Would you care to explain the equation I've written on the board?"

Vivian blinked and glanced at the digital board where a complex formula involving energy transference was projected. He knew the answer but didn't care enough to offer it. Instead, he shrugged.

The teacher sighed. "Try to stay focused."

Vivian slouched further into his seat, glancing at the clock. Another thirty minutes until this class was over, another four hours until school ended, another endless day in a life that was becoming increasingly difficult to tolerate. His classmates were busy with their group project—building what was supposed to be a "time machine." It was a joke, of course. No one really believed it would work. It was just an assignment to test their knowledge of quantum theory, a way to keep them busy.

"Hey, Viv!" came a whisper from the desk next to him.

It was Thalia, a girl who always seemed far too enthusiastic about everything. She had tied her curly hair up into a messy bun, her glasses perched precariously on the edge of her nose. She was practically bouncing in her seat. "Did you see what the others are doing? They're actually trying to get the machine to work."

Vivian barely turned his head. "What's the point? It's not going to work."

"You never know!" Thalia said with a grin. "Come on, where's your sense of adventure?"

"I think I lost it somewhere between math class and recess," Vivian muttered.

"You're such a downer lately. You used to love this stuff," Thalia said, her voice softening.

She was right, of course. He *used* to love it. The idea of time travel, of bending the laws of physics, of doing something impossible—that used to excite him. But now it felt like a distant memory.

"Well, if you change your mind, we're going to test it soon," she added with a wink, turning back to the group.

Vivian stared at the half-assembled machine in the center of the classroom. It was a mess of wires, circuits, and holographic interfaces. A ridiculous concoction of what his classmates thought a time machine should look like. It wasn't going to do anything. But still... something about it tugged at his attention.

What if it did work?

The thought was absurd. Time travel wasn't real. At least, not as far as anyone knew. But the idea of escaping—of breaking free from this tedious, predictable life—was tempting.

For the rest of the class, Vivian tried to ignore the gnawing thought in the back of his mind, but it wouldn't go away. What if there was a way out? What if this ridiculous machine could take him somewhere new? Somewhere impossible?

When the final bell rang, his classmates gathered around the machine, excitedly preparing for their so-called "experiment." Thalia waved him over, grinning like a mad scientist. "You've gotta see this, Viv! We're about to make history."

Vivian hesitated. He could just leave, go home to another evening of nothingness. Or he could take a risk, however silly it seemed, and see what happened.

Before he realized what he was doing, he found himself walking over to the group.

"Alright," Thalia said, practically buzzing with excitement. "We need someone to be the first volunteer. Any takers?"

Vivian looked around at the others. No one raised their hand. They were all excited, but none of them actually believed the machine would work. It was all just a game to them.

But to Vivian, it was starting to feel like something more.

"I'll do it," he said, his voice clear and steady.

The group fell silent, staring at him. Even Thalia looked shocked. "Really?" she asked, eyes wide.

"Yeah," Vivian said, surprising even himself. "Why not?"

Before anyone could stop him, he stepped forward and climbed into the small chamber at the center of the machine. It wasn't much bigger than a closet, with a glowing blue panel that looked like it was supposed to be some kind of control interface.

"Uh, Viv, you sure about this?" one of the boys asked, nervously glancing at the mess of wires. "It's not, like, dangerous or anything, but still..."

Vivian just shrugged. "What's the worst that could happen?"

He sat down in the chamber and pulled the door closed behind him. The world outside became muffled, and all he could hear was the low hum of the machine powering up. For a moment, nothing happened, and he started to wonder if it really was just a waste of time.

Then the lights flickered.

A strange vibration pulsed through the air, and suddenly, the machine began to whirr louder and louder. His classmates' voices turned into faint echoes, and the chamber grew warmer, the lights outside blurring into streaks of color.

Before Vivian could even process what was happening, the machine let out a deafening *whirrrr*, and everything around him went dark.

He wasn't in the classroom anymore.

Chapter 2: Into the Time Machine

The sensation of falling gripped Vivian's stomach as darkness enveloped him. It was an overwhelming emptiness, like drifting through the vacuum of space. No sound. No light. Just a black abyss that seemed to stretch on forever. His heart pounded in his chest as he reached out, but there was nothing to grab hold of—no solid ground, no walls.

For a moment, panic surged in his veins. Was this it? Was he stuck in this void forever?

Suddenly, a cold breeze brushed against his face, and something shifted in the air. Ahead, far in the distance, a faint glimmer of light appeared, growing brighter by the second. The sensation of falling stopped, and instead, he felt himself being pulled toward the light. Faster and faster, the tiny pinprick of brightness expanded, until it became a blinding flash that swallowed him whole.

The next thing Vivian knew, he was lying flat on his back, staring up at a swirling sky of deep purples and shimmering blues. Strange, wispy clouds floated above him, twisting and shifting in unnatural ways. His body felt heavy, almost like gravity was pulling him harder than usual.

"Ah, you're awake!" A cheery voice, startling in its suddenness, broke through the eerie quiet.

Vivian sat up, blinking against the strange colors that swirled around him. He was no longer in the classroom. That much was obvious. Instead, he found himself in a peculiar, vast room filled with bizarre machinery and glowing contraptions. It looked like something out of a science fiction movie, with pipes running along the walls, glowing orbs floating in midair, and strange symbols etched into the metal floor beneath him.

Standing nearby, in front of a large console with a collection of levers, buttons, and blinking lights, was a tall, eccentric-looking man. He wore a long, flowing coat that shimmered with the same colors as the sky above, and his wild, silver hair stuck out in all directions, giving him the appearance of someone who had just been struck by lightning. His round glasses reflected the glow of the machines, obscuring his eyes, but his wide grin was unmistakable.

"Welcome, my boy!" the man said, spreading his arms wide. "Welcome to the Infinite Nexus, the world where the impossible becomes possible!"

Vivian blinked, still disoriented. "What...what is this place? Where am I?"

The man strode forward, his coat billowing behind him as he walked. "You, my young friend, have arrived in a world where the ordinary rules of reality do not apply! Time, space, matter—here, they bend and twist to our will!" He stopped in front of Vivian, offering a gloved hand to help him up. "I am Professor Arcturus, and I must say, it's not often we get visitors from your dimension."

Vivian took the professor's hand, pulling himself to his feet. His legs wobbled slightly as he regained his balance. "Dimension?" he repeated, trying to process what was happening. "You mean...this isn't Earth?"

Professor Arcturus chuckled, the sound echoing through the vast chamber. "Oh, heavens no! You've traveled far beyond Earth, my boy. This is a world between worlds, a place where the very fabric of reality can be molded like clay."

Vivian's head spun with questions. "But...how? The time machine...it actually worked?"

"Ah, yes, your little contraption," the professor said, waving a hand dismissively. "A rather crude device, if I do say so myself. But it seems to have done the trick, hasn't it?" He grinned again, clearly amused by the situation. "I must admit, I didn't expect anyone from your world to actually stumble upon this place, but here you are!"

Vivian stared at the professor, his mind racing. "So...what is this place exactly? And how did I get here?"

Professor Arcturus's grin widened. "This, my boy, is the Infinite Nexus. It's a crossroads of sorts—an intersection of dimensions, if you will. A place where realities converge, and the laws of physics as you know them cease to exist." He gestured toward one of the machines, a towering structure made of gleaming metal and floating spheres. "Here, we have the ability to manipulate time, space, and even the fundamental forces of the universe. You've stepped into a world where science and magic are one and the same."

Vivian's eyes widened as he took in the strange, surreal surroundings. Floating orbs of light bobbed gently in the air, casting eerie shadows on the walls. Some of the machines seemed to hum with an otherworldly energy, and others made strange, melodic sounds that resonated deep in his chest.

"But...I don't understand," Vivian said, his voice trailing off. "How is any of this possible?"

"Ah, the classic question!" Professor Arcturus exclaimed, clapping his hands together. "You see, in your world, science is governed by a set of rigid rules. Laws of nature that cannot be broken. But here, we have learned to...shall we say...bend those rules. In this world, science and magic are not separate disciplines—they are one and the same. We call it 'impossible science.'" He winked, clearly proud of the term.

Vivian's mind reeled. "Impossible science?"

"Indeed!" the professor said, clearly delighted by Vivian's bewilderment. "Here, we use the building blocks of reality itself—time, energy, matter—to create things that would be considered impossible in your world. We can manipulate gravity, bend light, reshape time! You name it, we can do it."

Vivian couldn't believe what he was hearing. He had always thought of science as a series of logical steps, grounded in reality. But this place, this *world*, seemed to operate on entirely different principles. "So...you're saying that anything is possible here?"

"Precisely!" Professor Arcturus said, his eyes gleaming behind his glasses. "Anything you can imagine, we can create. The only limit is your mind."

Vivian's heart raced as he tried to wrap his head around what he was hearing. This was beyond anything he had ever imagined. In his world, everything had always felt so...limited. So ordinary. But here, in this strange new place, it felt like the very fabric of reality could be molded like clay.

For the first time in what felt like forever, a spark of excitement ignited within him. This was what he had been missing—what he had been longing for. A world where the impossible wasn't just possible, but real.

Professor Arcturus seemed to sense the shift in Vivian's mood, because he clapped him on the shoulder and gave him a knowing smile. "I can see you're starting to understand, my boy. But trust me, this is only the beginning. There's so much more to see, so much more to learn!"

He turned and walked over to a large, circular door that seemed to lead out of the chamber. With a flourish, he pressed a series of buttons on the console beside it, and the door slowly slid open, revealing a sprawling, breathtaking cityscape beyond. Towers of glass and metal stretched into the sky, their surfaces shimmering with strange, iridescent colors. Bridges of light connected the buildings, and in the distance, massive machines floated through the air, defying gravity with ease.

"Welcome to the City of Wonder," Professor Arcturus said, his voice filled with pride. "A place where the impossible is not only possible—it's the norm."

Vivian stepped forward, his breath catching in his throat as he took in the sight. The city was like nothing he had ever seen before. It was a place where science fiction met fantasy, where the laws of physics seemed more like suggestions than rules.

"Come," the professor said, beckoning him forward. "There's so much more to show you. This is just the beginning of your journey."

As they stepped through the doorway and into the heart of the city, Vivian felt a thrill of excitement rush through him. For the first time in his life, he felt like he was exactly where he was meant to be. A world of infinite possibilities lay before him, and he couldn't wait to see where it would take him.

Chapter 3: The New World

The moment Vivian stepped through the door, the sheer scale of the City of Wonder hit him like a gust of wind. Everywhere he looked, towering structures stretched toward the sky, their surfaces gleaming with an iridescent glow that shifted from blue to green to purple as the light struck them. It was as if the city were alive, constantly shifting and changing, just like the world around it. Everything seemed to defy logic—the streets were paved with a substance that shimmered and rippled underfoot, and overhead, machines floated effortlessly, their large mechanical wings catching the breeze in a way that made them seem almost like living creatures.

The city hummed with an energy that felt alive. Strange melodies echoed from unknown sources, and the air smelled faintly of ozone, mixed with the scent of something sweet and metallic.

Vivian's mouth hung open as he took it all in. "This place...it's amazing."

Professor Arcturus chuckled beside him. "Ah, yes. The City of Wonder has that effect on first-time visitors. Even I never grow tired of it, and I've lived here for quite some time."

"How is any of this possible?" Vivian asked, his eyes wide as a floating platform glided past them, carrying a group of people who appeared to be deep in conversation, as though soaring through the air was the most ordinary thing in the world.

"Well, my boy, it all comes down to a principle we call 'Quantum Flux Manipulation,'" the professor explained, clearly delighted by Vivian's awe. "Here in the Nexus, we've discovered that the building blocks of reality—space, time, energy—are much more malleable than in your world. Using a combination of advanced science and a little bit of magic, we've learned how to control and reshape these elements to create...well, anything."

He gestured to a series of bridges that hung in the air, each one formed from streams of light that bent and shifted, as though they were alive. "Take those bridges, for example. They're made from photons, particles of light, held together by a gravitational field that we can manipulate at will."

Vivian stared, speechless, as someone walked across one of the light bridges, their feet glowing as they moved. "This is...impossible."

"Not impossible," the professor corrected with a grin. "Just...unexpected."

They walked deeper into the city, and Vivian's mind continued to whirl with questions. Around them, the buildings twisted in ways that shouldn't have been possible, bending and curving in strange, gravity-defying angles. Some were shaped like spirals that seemed to wind infinitely upward, while others hovered just above the ground, as though they were suspended in the air by some unseen force.

But what amazed Vivian even more were the people. They walked casually through the streets, completely unfazed by the surreal world around them. Some wore glowing suits that allowed them to fly effortlessly between buildings, while others carried small devices that projected holographic screens in front of them. There were even a few people who appeared to be conducting experiments right there in the open, manipulating the fabric of reality with simple gestures and strange tools.

"Are they all scientists?" Vivian asked as they passed a group of people who were debating something over a series of floating equations.

"Oh, not at all," the professor replied. "Here in the Nexus, everyone has access to the same knowledge and tools, regardless of their background. Some are scientists, yes, but others are artists, philosophers, or even just curious explorers. The beauty of this world is that the boundaries between disciplines have blurred. Science, magic, art—they all work together here."

Vivian nodded, though it was still hard for him to wrap his head around the idea of science and magic being the same thing. In his world, they were always presented as opposites. Science was rational, predictable. Magic was chaotic, impossible. But here, they seemed to blend together seamlessly.

As they walked, the professor led Vivian to the edge of the city, where the buildings gave way to a vast open landscape. In the distance, Vivian could see strange floating islands, each one suspended in the air by invisible forces. Some of the islands were covered in lush green forests, while others housed bizarre structures that looked like they belonged in a dream.

"What are those?" Vivian asked, pointing to the islands.

"Ah, those are the Islands of Impossibility," Professor Arcturus explained. "Each one contains its own unique environment and set of rules. Some operate on different laws of physics, while others are home to creatures that couldn't possibly exist in your world."

"Creatures?" Vivian asked, his curiosity piqued.

"Oh, yes," the professor said with a gleam in his eye. "Would you like to see one?"

Vivian nodded eagerly, and the professor grinned. "Very well. Follow me."

They made their way to a nearby platform that hovered just off the ground. The professor stepped onto it, and with a gesture, the platform began to rise into the air, carrying them toward one of the floating islands. As they ascended, Vivian's heart raced with excitement. This was exactly what he had been craving—something new, something exciting. An adventure.

When they reached the island, Vivian gasped. It was a sprawling jungle, filled with plants and trees unlike anything he had ever seen. The foliage glowed faintly in the twilight, casting an otherworldly light over the landscape. Strange, luminescent flowers bloomed in every direction, and the air was filled with the soft hum of insects and birds—though these creatures were unlike any animals Vivian had encountered back on Earth.

A large bird-like creature with iridescent feathers flew past them, its wings making no sound as it glided effortlessly through the trees. Its eyes glowed a soft blue, and as it passed, the very air around it seemed to shimmer.

"That's a Quantum Sparrow," the professor said, nodding toward the bird. "Its feathers are made from condensed quantum particles, which allow it to bend light around itself. Quite a beautiful creature, isn't it?"

Vivian nodded, staring in wonder at the sparrow as it disappeared into the trees.

"Come along," the professor said, leading him deeper into the jungle. "There's something even more fascinating I want to show you."

They walked for several minutes through the glowing jungle, the plants rustling softly as they moved. The air was cool and crisp, and Vivian felt a strange sense of calm wash over him. For the first time in what felt like years, he wasn't bored. In fact, he felt more alive than ever.

Finally, they reached a small clearing where a peculiar creature stood, quietly observing them with curious eyes. It was about the size of a dog, with sleek, silver fur that shimmered in the light. Its ears were long and pointed, and its eyes glowed a faint gold. But the most striking thing about it was the fact that it seemed to flicker in and out of existence, as though it were phasing between two different realities.

"This," Professor Arcturus said with pride, "is a Chronofox. A creature native to this island, capable of slipping between moments in time. Fascinating, isn't it?"

Vivian stared in awe. "It can travel through time?"

"Not in the way you're thinking," the professor explained. "It doesn't travel to the past or the future—it simply exists in multiple moments at once. It can shift slightly between different timelines, giving it the ability to dodge attacks or move between spaces without being seen."

As if on cue, the Chronofox flickered and reappeared a few feet away, staring at them with its golden eyes.

Vivian took a cautious step forward, his heart pounding in his chest. He had never seen anything like this before. The Chronofox tilted its head, watching him closely, but it didn't run. Slowly, Vivian extended his hand toward it.

To his amazement, the creature stepped forward, gently nuzzling his hand with its cold, wet nose. Vivian felt a thrill of excitement as the Chronofox's fur flickered beneath his touch, its body phasing in and out of existence.

"It likes you," the professor said with a smile. "Quite rare for a Chronofox to trust someone so quickly."

Vivian couldn't help but smile as the creature leaned into his hand. "This place...it's incredible," he said, his voice filled with wonder.

Professor Arcturus nodded. "And this is just the beginning, my boy. There is so much more for you to see, to learn. This world is filled with impossible wonders, and I believe you're destined to discover them."

For the first time in his life, Vivian felt like he was exactly where he belonged. This world, with its strange creatures and impossible science, was the adventure he had always dreamed of. And he couldn't wait to see what came next.

Chapter 4: The City of Wonder

The floating platform hummed softly beneath Vivian's feet as he and Professor Arcturus soared back toward the heart of the City of Wonder. Below them, the glowing jungle and floating islands slowly faded from view, replaced by the glittering expanse of the city. Vivian couldn't tear his eyes away from the sight—so many impossible things, each one more unbelievable than the last.

"You're quite taken by it all, aren't you?" the professor remarked, watching Vivian with a knowing smile.

"How could I not be?" Vivian replied, shaking his head in disbelief. "This place...it's like a dream. But it feels so real."

"Oh, it's real, all right," the professor said. "Every impossible thing you see here is the result of centuries of exploration and discovery. The people of this world have unlocked the secrets of reality itself, and they've used that knowledge to create wonders that would seem like magic in your world."

Vivian nodded, still trying to process it all. Back home, science was always presented as a rigid set of rules—laws that couldn't be broken. But here, it was something entirely different. The people of the Nexus didn't see science as a limitation. They saw it as a tool to shape the world around them.

As they descended into the heart of the city, Vivian saw more examples of this limitless thinking. Tall, spiraling towers twisted in ways that shouldn't have been physically possible, their foundations hovering inches above the ground. Bridges of light connected buildings that floated in mid-air, shifting and changing shape as people walked across them. Even the streets seemed to have a life of their own, pulsing and rippling like the surface of a pond.

But it wasn't just the architecture that amazed him. The people themselves were just as extraordinary. They moved through the city with a casual ease, as though the impossible had become routine for them. Some wore suits that allowed them to glide effortlessly through the air, while others carried strange devices that emitted light and sound, projecting holographic images and streams of data.

One man walked past them, his body flickering in and out of existence as he adjusted a small, glowing dial on his wrist. Another woman was talking to a floating, metallic cube that responded in a language Vivian couldn't understand. Everywhere he looked, people were pushing the boundaries of what he had always thought was possible.

The platform came to a gentle stop in front of a large, domed building made entirely of shimmering glass. The dome pulsed faintly with light, and as they stepped off the platform, the surface of the building rippled like water, allowing them to pass through.

"Welcome to the Nexus Institute of Impossible Sciences," Professor Arcturus said proudly. "This is where the greatest minds of our world gather to unlock the secrets of the universe."

Vivian's eyes widened as he looked around. Inside the dome, the space seemed even larger than it had from the outside. Dozens of platforms floated in mid-air, each one occupied by a team of researchers working on some strange, futuristic device. Holographic screens filled the air, displaying equations and diagrams that made Vivian's head spin. In one corner of the room, a group of scientists appeared to be manipulating a miniature black hole, its swirling mass contained within a glass sphere. In another area, a pair of researchers were examining a creature that looked like a cross between a lion and a dragon, its scales shifting colors as it breathed.

"This is where we conduct our most important experiments," the professor explained. "Time travel, gravity manipulation, molecular restructuring—it all happens here. Every discovery we make brings us one step closer to understanding the true nature of reality."

Vivian could hardly believe what he was seeing. "So...anyone can come here and just do this? Play with black holes? Mess with time?"

"Not quite," the professor said with a chuckle. "There's a certain...etiquette, let's say. You must have a solid understanding of the rules before you can bend them. But once you do, the possibilities are endless."

They walked through the massive chamber, passing by researchers who were deep in conversation, their hands moving in intricate patterns as they manipulated light, energy, and matter in ways Vivian had never imagined. In one section, a group of engineers was building what appeared to be a teleportation gate, its swirling energy field sparking with flashes of light. In another, a man was conducting an experiment with what looked like a floating orb of water, pulling and shaping the liquid into different forms with nothing but a few gestures.

Vivian's mind raced as he tried to make sense of it all. This wasn't just about breaking the laws of physics. It was about rewriting them.

"Here," Professor Arcturus said, leading him toward a central platform. "I want to show you something special."

They stepped onto the platform, and in an instant, the floor beneath them rose into the air, carrying them to a higher level of the dome. As they ascended, the city outside became visible through the transparent walls, the glowing skyline stretching out in every direction.

When they reached the top, the platform stopped, and in front of them stood a large, crystalline structure that pulsed with a soft, blue light. It was shaped like an enormous diamond, hovering just above the platform's surface, and its facets reflected the city below in strange, distorted patterns.

"This," the professor said, gesturing toward the crystal, "is the Quantum Core. It's the heart of the Nexus—the source of the energy that powers our world."

Vivian stared at the crystal, mesmerized by the way it seemed to shift and pulse with an inner light. "How does it work?"

"Ah, that's the beauty of it," the professor said, his voice filled with admiration. "The Quantum Core draws its energy from the multiverse itself—tapping into the infinite potential of parallel dimensions. It's what allows us to bend the laws of physics, to reshape reality. Every impossible thing you've seen in this world is made possible by the energy of the Quantum Core."

Vivian took a step closer to the crystal, feeling the faint hum of its energy beneath his feet. "So...this is what makes everything here possible?"

"Exactly," Professor Arcturus said. "Without it, none of this would exist."

Vivian stood in silence for a moment, staring at the crystal. The idea that something so small could have so much power was almost too much to comprehend. Back home, energy came from the sun, from power plants, from predictable, limited sources. But here, the energy came from something far greater—something infinite.

The professor gave him a moment to take it all in before placing a hand on Vivian's shoulder. "Come. There's still much more to see."

They descended back into the main chamber, where the researchers continued their work, seemingly oblivious to the awe-inspiring world around them. For them, this was normal. But for Vivian, it was the most extraordinary thing he had ever experienced.

As they left the Institute and stepped back into the streets of the city, Vivian found himself lost in thought. He had always dreamed of finding something more—something beyond the ordinary, predictable life he had known back home. And now, here it was. A world where anything was possible, where the only limit was his imagination.

But as he looked around at the people of the Nexus, going about their lives with such casual ease, he couldn't help but wonder—what was it like to live in a place like this? Did they ever grow tired of it? Did the impossible ever become...mundane?

"Professor," Vivian said hesitantly, "doesn't anyone here...get bored? I mean, when everything's possible, doesn't that take away the excitement?"

The professor smiled knowingly. "Ah, you're beginning to see the dilemma, aren't you? Yes, my boy, even in a world of infinite possibilities, there are those who struggle to find meaning. When you can bend reality to your will, the challenge lies not in discovering what's possible, but in choosing what matters."

Vivian frowned. "What do you mean?"

"The people of the Nexus have unlocked the secrets of the universe," the professor explained. "But in doing so, they've also realized that the real challenge isn't in what you can do, but in what you choose to do. With so many options, so many paths to take, it's easy to lose sight of what's truly important."

Vivian thought about that for a moment. He had come here looking for excitement, for adventure. But now he was beginning to see that even in a place like this, where the impossible was possible, people still had to make choices. They still had to find their purpose.

"That's why I brought you here," the professor continued, his tone growing serious. "Not just to show you the wonders of this world, but to help you understand something important. No matter how extraordinary a place may be, it's up to you to find your own meaning in it."

Vivian nodded slowly, the professor's words sinking in. He had spent so much time feeling trapped by the monotony of his life back home. But maybe, just maybe, the answers he was looking for weren't in the world around him. Maybe they were inside him all along.

The professor gave him a gentle pat on the shoulder. "Come along, my boy. There's much more for you to discover."

As they walked deeper into the city, Vivian couldn't shake the feeling that his journey had only just begun.

Chapter 5: Learning the Magic of Science

The city had left Vivian breathless, but now, within the confines of Professor Arcturus' personal workshop, his excitement was shifting into something more focused—something that felt like a burning curiosity. He had spent most of his life feeling like the world around him was already explored, every corner understood, every question already answered. Here, in this strange place, it was as if the universe itself had opened its doors and invited him in to see its secrets.

The professor's workshop was nothing like the sprawling laboratory of the Nexus Institute. It was smaller, cozier, filled with half-finished machines, glowing blueprints suspended in mid-air, and shelves crammed with strange devices that hummed softly, as if they were alive. The air was thick with the scent of metal and ozone, mixed with something sweet and unfamiliar.

"This is where I do my best thinking," Professor Arcturus said, gesturing to the cluttered room. "The Nexus Institute is fine for formal research, but here, I'm free to experiment in ways that aren't...bound by the usual protocols."

Vivian ran his fingers over a device that looked like a cross between a telescope and a violin, its surface etched with glowing runes. "What does this do?"

The professor glanced at it and smiled. "Ah, that's one of my older inventions—a Harmonium Scope. It uses sound waves to bend light, allowing you to see through objects. Quite useful for finding things that tend to disappear into other dimensions."

Vivian blinked. "Other dimensions?"

"Indeed!" the professor said, flipping a switch on a nearby panel. A holographic projection of a swirling mass of colors appeared in front of them. "Here in the Nexus, we're not limited to just one reality. There are countless dimensions, each with its own unique properties. Some are similar to yours, others are...well, rather strange. Time moves differently in some, gravity works backward in others. It's all quite fascinating, really."

"Do people here travel between dimensions a lot?" Vivian asked, still struggling to wrap his head around the concept.

"Only when necessary," the professor replied. "Navigating between dimensions requires a delicate balance of science and magic, and it can be rather dangerous if you don't know what you're doing. But it's essential for understanding the true nature of the universe."

Vivian stared at the swirling colors of the holographic projection, his mind racing. "So...can anyone learn how to do this? I mean, could I?"

Professor Arcturus grinned. "That's exactly what I was hoping you'd ask."

He walked over to a nearby table, where a small device sat glowing faintly. It looked like a miniature version of the crystal structure they had seen at the Nexus Institute—the Quantum Core—but this one was no larger than Vivian's fist.

"This," the professor said, picking up the device, "is a Quantum Spark. It's a smaller, more focused version of the Quantum Core, designed to power individual experiments. With this, you can manipulate the basic elements of reality in controlled ways."

He handed the Quantum Spark to Vivian, who held it carefully, feeling the faint pulse of energy beneath his fingertips. "So...what can I do with it?"

"That depends on you," the professor said. "The Quantum Spark responds to your thoughts, your intentions. It draws energy from the multiverse, allowing you to reshape the world around you. But be careful—without focus and discipline, it can be unpredictable."

Vivian felt a thrill of excitement surge through him. For the first time, he wasn't just an observer in this world. He was part of it. He could *do* things, change things.

The professor led him to a large, open space in the center of the workshop, where a series of objects were laid out—metallic cubes, glass orbs, and small devices that hummed faintly. "Start with something simple," the professor suggested. "Try lifting one of these cubes. Focus on the Quantum Spark, and imagine the energy flowing through it."

Vivian nodded, feeling his heart race as he held the Quantum Spark tightly in his hand. He stared at one of the metallic cubes, willing it to rise. For a moment, nothing happened. Then, slowly, the cube began to vibrate. A faint glow surrounded it, and with a soft *whir*, it lifted off the ground, hovering a few feet in the air.

"I did it!" Vivian gasped, his eyes wide with amazement.

"Indeed you did!" the professor said, clapping his hands. "Well done, my boy!"

Vivian grinned, feeling a surge of pride. This wasn't like anything he had ever experienced back home. There, everything had felt so limited, so controlled. But here, the world was open, flexible, ready to be shaped by his imagination.

"Now," the professor said, "try something a bit more advanced. See if you can split the cube into smaller pieces."

Vivian frowned, focusing on the cube. He imagined it breaking apart, splitting into smaller sections, and to his amazement, the cube began to glow brighter. A soft *crackling* sound filled the air as the cube divided into four smaller pieces, each one hovering independently in front of him.

"This is incredible," Vivian whispered, staring at the floating pieces. He felt like he could do anything.

"Careful now," the professor warned, his tone serious. "It's easy to get carried away with the possibilities, but remember—everything you do here has consequences. The energy you're manipulating comes from the multiverse itself. If you lose control, it can become...unpredictable."

Vivian nodded, suddenly feeling the weight of what he was holding. This wasn't just a toy. It was power—real, tangible power.

"Let's try something different," the professor said, gesturing to one of the glass orbs on the table. "This orb is designed to contain energy in its raw form. I want you to transfer some of the Quantum Spark's energy into it. But be careful—the orb can only hold so much before it overloads."

Vivian took a deep breath, focusing on the glass orb. He felt the Quantum Spark pulse in his hand, its energy flowing through him. Slowly, he extended his hand toward the orb, willing the energy to transfer.

At first, the orb glowed softly, its surface shimmering with a faint light. But as more energy flowed into it, the glow intensified, and cracks began to appear along its surface.

"Steady now," the professor said, his eyes narrowing. "Too much, and the orb will shatter."

Vivian gritted his teeth, trying to maintain control, but the energy seemed to have a will of its own. The orb glowed brighter and brighter, the cracks spreading like spiderwebs across its surface.

"Stop!" the professor shouted.

But it was too late. With a deafening *crack*, the orb exploded, sending shards of glass flying in every direction. Vivian staggered backward, shielding his face with his arms as a wave of energy rippled through the room.

When the dust settled, Vivian lowered his arms, breathing heavily. The glass orb was gone, replaced by a small cloud of shimmering particles that hovered in the air, slowly dissipating.

"I...I'm sorry," Vivian said, his voice shaky. "I didn't mean to—"

"No harm done," the professor said, waving a hand dismissively. "That's the nature of experimentation, my boy. You learn by making mistakes. But now you understand the importance of control. Power without focus is dangerous."

Vivian nodded, still feeling the rush of energy coursing through him. The thrill of creating, of shaping the world around him, was intoxicating. But he also realized the truth of what the professor had said. This wasn't just a game. The Quantum Spark held real power, and with it came real responsibility.

The professor smiled, placing a hand on his shoulder. "You did well, Vivian. Very well. It takes most people weeks to even begin to understand the Quantum Spark, but you've already shown great promise. There's much more for you to learn, but I believe you're ready for the next step."

Vivian's heart raced. "What's the next step?"

Professor Arcturus's smile widened. "We're going to create something truly impossible."

Chapter 6: A World of Infinite Possibilities

The workshop hummed with an electric energy as Professor Arcturus adjusted the strange contraption in front of him. It was unlike anything Vivian had seen before—an intricate web of glowing wires and pulsing crystals, all suspended in midair by invisible forces. The machine radiated power, its surface flickering with arcs of blue and white light, casting strange shadows around the room.

"Now," the professor said, turning to Vivian with a glint in his eye, "what we're about to do here is no ordinary experiment. This will be your first taste of true creation—a chance to harness the Quantum Spark and bend reality itself."

Vivian's heart raced with anticipation. He had already learned to manipulate small objects, to lift them and even split them apart, but this felt like something far greater. The power pulsing from the machine was almost tangible, like it was alive.

"What are we creating?" Vivian asked, unable to tear his eyes away from the device.

Professor Arcturus smiled. "We're going to create a pocket dimension—a small, self-contained reality that exists outside of the normal rules of space and time. In this dimension, you will have full control. You can shape it however you like, filling it with whatever impossible things you can imagine."

Vivian's breath caught in his throat. "A whole dimension? I can create that?"

"Yes, but remember," the professor said, raising a finger, "creation is a delicate process. While the Quantum Spark gives you the power to bend reality, it requires focus and intent. The more detailed and vivid your imagination, the stronger and more stable the dimension will be."

Vivian felt a surge of excitement. This was beyond anything he had imagined when he first arrived in the Nexus. He had always dreamed of exploring strange new worlds, but now he had the chance to create one himself.

The professor gestured to the glowing machine. "Go ahead. Step up to the console and place your hand on the control crystal. Let the Quantum Spark guide you."

Vivian nodded, taking a deep breath as he approached the console. The control crystal glowed with a soft, inviting light, and as he reached out and placed his hand on it, he felt a surge of energy rush through his body. The Quantum Spark in his other hand pulsed in response, syncing with the machine as it hummed to life.

For a moment, nothing happened. Then, slowly, a faint image began to take shape in the air in front of him. It was like looking at a foggy mirror, the outline of a swirling, undefined space hovering in midair.

"Now," the professor said softly, "focus. Picture the world you want to create. Imagine every detail—the landscape, the sky, the creatures that live there. Let your mind guide the energy."

Vivian closed his eyes, his heart pounding. He imagined a vast, open field, filled with tall, golden grass that swayed in the breeze. Above it, a sky of deep violet stretched endlessly, dotted with glowing stars. He could see rolling hills in the distance, and beyond them, towering mountains that sparkled like crystals in the twilight. Strange, glowing trees lined the horizon, their branches bending in impossible shapes.

As the image formed in his mind, he felt the energy around him pulse, responding to his thoughts. The swirling fog in front of him began to solidify, taking on the shapes and colors he had imagined.

When Vivian opened his eyes, he gasped. There, in front of him, was the very world he had envisioned—a shimmering pocket dimension, suspended in midair. It was like looking through a window into another reality, a miniature version of the world he had just created.

"I did it," Vivian whispered, his voice filled with wonder.

"You did indeed," the professor said, beaming with pride. "And a fine creation it is."

Vivian reached out, his hand hovering just above the surface of the pocket dimension. It felt real, solid, as though he could step through the window and into the world beyond. The golden grass swayed gently in the breeze, just as he had imagined it, and the glowing trees cast soft, otherworldly shadows.

"This is amazing," Vivian said, his eyes wide. "It's...perfect."

The professor nodded. "But remember, my boy, this is just the beginning. Pocket dimensions like this are small, stable creations. But there are far greater dimensions out there—entire realities, each with its own set of rules, its own possibilities. The multiverse is vast, and you've only scratched the surface."

Vivian felt his pulse quicken. The idea that there were infinite worlds out there, each one with its own unique laws of nature, filled him with a sense of awe. Back home, everything had felt so limited, so predictable. But here, the possibilities were endless.

"How do I learn to create bigger ones?" Vivian asked, eager to push the limits of what he could do.

"Patience," the professor said, raising a hand. "Creation is not just about power—it's about understanding. The multiverse is vast and complex, and each reality has its own unique structure. If you're not careful, you could create something unstable, something that could unravel itself—or worse."

Vivian nodded, a chill running down his spine. He hadn't considered the risks, but he could see now that this power, as thrilling as it was, required caution.

"But you have the potential," the professor added, his tone reassuring. "In time, you will learn to shape greater realities, to bend the laws of physics and time itself. But for now, let's focus on controlling the basics."

Vivian turned back to the pocket dimension, his mind racing. He could see the potential—the endless possibilities that lay ahead. But he also understood the weight of what he was learning. This wasn't just about creating worlds for fun. There was a deeper, more profound responsibility here.

"Are there other people who can do this?" Vivian asked, stepping back from the console.

The professor nodded. "Oh, yes. There are others like you—individuals who have learned to harness the power of the Quantum Spark, to create and explore new dimensions. Some use their abilities for discovery, for expanding the boundaries of knowledge. Others..." He trailed off, his expression darkening for a moment. "Well, let's just say not everyone has the same noble intentions."

Vivian frowned. "You mean, there are people who use this power for...bad things?"

The professor sighed. "The multiverse is a place of infinite possibilities, and with that comes infinite choices. Some seek to manipulate entire realities for their own gain. Others create unstable dimensions that threaten to spill over into our world, wreaking havoc. It's a dangerous game, my boy, and not everyone plays by the rules."

Vivian felt a knot form in his stomach. He had thought this world was a place of wonder, of discovery. But now he was beginning to see that even here, there were dangers—real, serious dangers.

"That's why it's important for you to learn control," the professor said, his voice steady. "Power without control leads to chaos. But with discipline, with focus, you can create wonders that will inspire generations."

Vivian nodded slowly, feeling the weight of the professor's words. He had been so excited by the possibilities, by the idea of bending reality to his will, that he hadn't considered the consequences. But now he understood. This wasn't just about power. It was about responsibility.

The professor smiled gently. "Don't worry, my boy. You're learning quickly, and you have a good heart. That's the most important thing. As long as you remain mindful of the consequences, you'll do great things."

Vivian felt a wave of determination wash over him. He had come here looking for something more—something beyond the dull, predictable life he had left behind. And now, he had found it. But he also realized that this was about more than just escape. This was about discovery, about creation, and about understanding the infinite possibilities that lay before him.

"Are you ready for the next lesson?" the professor asked, raising an eyebrow.

Vivian smiled. "I'm ready."

Chapter 7: The Fantastical Creatures of Science

The next few days in the Nexus blurred by in a whirlwind of discovery. Every hour brought something new—an impossible invention, a creature that defied all logic, or a scientific concept that twisted reality into knots. But among all these wonders, what fascinated Vivian the most were the creatures of this world.

On the third day of his apprenticeship under Professor Arcturus, the professor had taken him to the *Menagerie of Impossibility*, a massive dome where creatures engineered through a blend of science and magic lived and thrived. The moment they entered, Vivian felt like he had stepped into the pages of an ancient myth, except here, the creatures were real—living, breathing marvels of impossible science.

"Welcome to the Menagerie," Professor Arcturus said as they walked into the vast, open expanse. Around them, glowing orbs floated in the air, casting a soft light over the vibrant landscape within the dome. "This is where we study and create life forms that wouldn't—or shouldn't—exist in any other reality."

Vivian's eyes widened as he took in the sight of the creatures around them. In the distance, a massive, serpentine creature with iridescent scales coiled around a floating rock, its body shimmering with energy. Nearby, a herd of small, rabbit-like animals hopped through the air, their fur glowing with faint, bioluminescent light.

"They're incredible," Vivian whispered, his voice filled with awe.

"Indeed," the professor said with a nod. "Each of these creatures was created using a blend of scientific principles and magical energies. Some are hybrids of species from different dimensions, while others are entirely new creations—creatures born from the imagination and ingenuity of our researchers."

As they walked further into the dome, Vivian noticed a large, open area where several researchers were gathered around a strange, crystalline creature that hovered a few feet above the ground. It was shaped like a lion, but its body was translucent, made entirely of crystal, and inside its chest, a pulsing core of energy glowed brightly.

"That's a Luminalis," the professor explained, nodding toward the creature. "A creature made entirely of light and crystal. Its core is a small fragment of the Quantum Spark, giving it the ability to manipulate light and gravity around it. Quite a majestic creature, wouldn't you agree?"

Vivian stared in awe as the Luminalis prowled gracefully through the air, its body shimmering with every movement. "How do you even create something like that?"

"The process is complex," the professor said, "but it all comes down to understanding the building blocks of life—how to manipulate matter and energy at the most fundamental levels. Here in the Nexus, we've unlocked the secrets of life itself, allowing us to create creatures that defy the natural order of things."

They continued their tour, passing by creatures that seemed to belong in the wildest fantasies of humanity—winged serpents that sang in musical tones, creatures with bodies made of water that could shift and flow like rivers, and others that moved through the air like ghosts, their forms constantly shifting and changing.

"Can anyone create creatures like these?" Vivian asked, marveling at the diversity of life around them.

"Yes and no," the professor replied. "The ability to create life requires a deep understanding of both science and magic. It's not just about imagination; it's about precision, control. Life is delicate, and one wrong step can lead to disastrous consequences."

Vivian frowned, sensing the seriousness in the professor's tone. "Has anything ever gone wrong?"

Professor Arcturus sighed, his expression growing somber. "Yes. Not everyone in the Nexus shares the same sense of responsibility. Some have tried to create life without fully understanding the consequences, and the results have been...unstable. There are creatures that roam the Nexus even now—beings born from failed experiments, their very existence a threat to the balance of reality."

Vivian's stomach tightened. He had seen the wonders of creation, but he hadn't considered the dangers. It was easy to get swept up in the excitement of the impossible, but there were risks—risks that could have catastrophic consequences.

The professor must have sensed his unease because he placed a reassuring hand on Vivian's shoulder. "But that's why we study. That's why we learn control. With knowledge and responsibility, you can create wonders that will inspire generations. But without it...well, that's a lesson for another time."

They walked deeper into the Menagerie, and Vivian couldn't help but feel a mixture of awe and apprehension. The creatures here were beautiful, majestic, but the professor's words hung in the back of his mind. The power to create was thrilling, but it came with a weight—a responsibility that he hadn't fully grasped until now.

As they rounded a corner, Vivian noticed a familiar face. The Chronofox—the small, time-bending creature he had encountered earlier—was sitting near a pond, its silver fur glinting in the soft light. It flickered in and out of existence, as though it was phasing between moments in time.

"Ah, your friend," the professor said with a smile. "It seems the Chronofox has taken a liking to you."

Vivian knelt down, holding out his hand. The Chronofox flickered again before stepping forward and nuzzling against his palm. Its fur was cool to the touch, like the surface of water, and as it moved, Vivian could feel the faint ripple of time around it.

"These creatures are born with the ability to manipulate time in small ways," the professor explained. "It's a natural defense mechanism, allowing them to slip in and out of different moments to avoid predators. Quite a remarkable species, though difficult to study."

Vivian smiled, feeling a sense of connection with the creature. There was something about the Chronofox—its quiet grace, its ability to move through time—that resonated with him. In a world where everything seemed bound by rules and limitations, the Chronofox lived outside of them, moving freely through moments in a way that defied all logic.

As he stroked the creature's fur, Vivian's mind wandered. What if he could learn to control time, just as the Chronofox did? What if he could manipulate moments, change outcomes, bend time to his will?

The thought was intoxicating. He had already learned to create, to shape reality. But the power to control time itself—that was something far greater. With that power, he could rewrite the past, undo mistakes, reshape the future.

"You're thinking about time, aren't you?" the professor said, his voice interrupting Vivian's thoughts.

Vivian glanced up, startled. "I guess I am. Is it...possible? To control time?"

The professor smiled, though there was a hint of sadness in his eyes. "Time is one of the most elusive forces in the multiverse. It can be bent, manipulated in small ways, as the Chronofox does. But true control over time—moving backward and forward, rewriting the past—that's a power even the most skilled among us struggle to grasp."

Vivian's heart sank slightly. "So it's impossible?"

"Not impossible," the professor said softly. "But dangerous. Time is fragile, my boy. It's the thread that binds reality together. Pull too hard on that thread, and the whole fabric of existence can unravel."

Vivian nodded slowly, the weight of the professor's words sinking in. He had seen the wonders of creation, but he had also glimpsed the dangers—the risks that came with manipulating the very forces of reality. Time, it seemed, was the most dangerous of all.

But even as the professor warned him, Vivian couldn't help but feel a sense of wonder. The Chronofox lived outside the normal flow of time, slipping between moments with ease. If such a small creature could do it, what could *he* accomplish with the right understanding, the right control?

As they left the Menagerie, Vivian's mind buzzed with possibilities. The world around him was filled with wonders—creatures born from impossible science, dimensions that bent the laws of reality. But it was more than that. It was a world of infinite possibilities, where the only limits were the ones he set for himself.

For the first time in his life, Vivian felt like he was part of something bigger than himself. He had come to the Nexus looking for escape, for adventure. But now, he realized, he was on a journey of discovery—not just of the world around him, but of his own potential.

And the deeper he went, the more he understood that this was only the beginning.

Chapter 8: The Rise of the Unseen

It started with a whisper.

The sound was faint, like the softest breeze rustling through leaves, but in the Nexus, even the smallest sound could carry the weight of something monumental. Vivian was sitting in Professor Arcturus's workshop, studying a series of notes on dimension-folding, when he first heard it—a strange, melodic hum that seemed to come from everywhere and nowhere at once.

At first, he thought it was another of the professor's devices malfunctioning. The workshop was filled with strange machines, many of which had a habit of coming to life in unexpected ways. But as the hum grew louder, Vivian realized it was something different—something far older, and far more mysterious.

"Do you hear that?" Vivian asked, glancing up from the floating holograms in front of him.

Professor Arcturus, who had been tinkering with a small device that resembled a watch, paused and tilted his head, listening. "Ah," he said quietly, his voice carrying a hint of both admiration and caution. "It seems the Unseen are stirring."

"The Unseen?" Vivian repeated, confused. "What are they?"

The professor put down his tools, his expression growing serious. "The Unseen are beings that exist between realities—creatures born from the spaces where the laws of the multiverse overlap and fracture. They're not quite alive in the way we understand life, but they're not entirely inanimate either. They're the embodiment of possibility, of potential, existing in the shadows of reality."

Vivian's heart quickened. "Are they dangerous?"

"Not usually," the professor said. "They tend to stay in their own realm, feeding off the ambient energy of the Nexus. But when they stir...well, it usually means they've sensed something—a shift in the balance of reality."

Vivian frowned. "A shift? What kind of shift?"

Professor Arcturus's eyes darkened. "Something is pulling them out of their hidden realm. It could be a disturbance in one of the dimensions, or perhaps someone has been tampering with forces they don't fully understand."

Vivian felt a knot tighten in his stomach. He had seen the wonders of creation, but he had also been warned of the dangers—the risks that came with manipulating the forces of the multiverse. Could this be one of those dangers?

The hum grew louder, reverberating through the workshop, and Vivian felt a strange sensation—like something was brushing against the edge of his consciousness, trying to make contact.

"Stay close," the professor said, his voice calm but firm. "We need to investigate. The Unseen rarely interact with our world unless something significant is happening."

They stepped out of the workshop and into the heart of the city. The humming sound followed them, growing in intensity, and the air itself seemed to shimmer with a faint, ethereal glow. People in the streets looked up, their faces filled with curiosity and unease. It was as if the very fabric of the Nexus was vibrating with potential, like a string pulled taut, ready to snap.

"Where are we going?" Vivian asked, his voice barely audible over the strange sound that now filled the air.

"To the Edge," the professor replied. "It's where the boundaries between realities are thinnest. If the Unseen are stirring, that's where we'll find them."

They moved quickly through the city, weaving between towering buildings and floating platforms, until they reached the outskirts—a place where the city's glow faded, giving way to an open, empty space that stretched into infinity. It was called the Edge, but it wasn't really an edge at all. There was no clear boundary, just a vast, shifting expanse where reality began to blur, and the sky above twisted in strange, fractal patterns.

Vivian felt a strange pull as they approached the Edge, like gravity itself was tugging at him in different directions. The ground beneath his feet seemed to ripple with every step, and in the distance, he could see shapes—vague, ghostly forms that flickered in and out of existence, like shadows cast by a flame that didn't exist.

"The Unseen," Professor Arcturus said, pointing toward the shapes. "They exist just outside our perception, in a realm that overlaps with ours but doesn't fully connect. But they're coming closer."

Vivian squinted, trying to make out the shapes. They were faint at first, like silhouettes of creatures that hadn't yet decided what form they wanted to take. As he watched, one of the shapes solidified, taking the form of a large, bird-like creature with wings made of shimmering mist. It hovered in the air, watching them with eyes that glowed faintly.

"What do they want?" Vivian asked, his voice barely above a whisper.

"That's the question," the professor replied. "The Unseen are drawn to disturbances in the fabric of reality, but they don't interact with our world unless something pulls them in. Whatever it is, it's powerful."

As they approached the Edge, the air grew colder, and the hum became a low, resonant vibration that Vivian could feel in his bones. The Unseen gathered around them, their forms shifting and changing—some taking on the shapes of animals, others resembling twisted versions of people, their faces obscured by a haze of mist and shadow.

And then, from the center of the gathering, a figure stepped forward.

It wasn't like the others. This figure was solid, its form fully defined. It looked like a person—a man, tall and lean, with dark, flowing robes and a face hidden beneath a hood. But there was something wrong about him, something off. His movements were too smooth, too precise, and the air around him shimmered with an unnatural energy.

The professor's eyes narrowed. "That's no ordinary Unseen," he said quietly. "That's someone using the power of the Unseen for their own purposes."

The figure raised its hand, and the hum in the air grew louder, vibrating through the ground beneath their feet. Vivian took a step back, his heart racing. The figure's hand glowed with a strange, ethereal light, and the Unseen creatures around them began to react, their forms flickering faster, as if they were being drawn toward the figure.

"You feel it, don't you?" the figure said, his voice echoing as though it were coming from multiple places at once. "The power that flows through this place—the power to reshape reality itself. The Unseen are not bound by the laws of your world. They are pure potential, and with them, I will create a new order."

The professor stepped forward, his expression calm but determined. "You're meddling with forces you don't understand. The Unseen aren't just tools for creation—they're the embodiment of everything that could go wrong. If you lose control, they'll tear the fabric of reality apart."

The figure chuckled, a low, menacing sound. "I have control. I understand the multiverse in ways you never could. I see the paths that others are too afraid to walk."

Vivian felt a surge of fear. The air around them was thick with energy, and the Unseen were gathering closer, their forms becoming more tangible, more real. The figure raised his hand again, and the shimmering energy around him pulsed, sending a shockwave through the ground.

"What do we do?" Vivian asked, his voice tight with fear.

The professor's gaze never wavered. "We have to disrupt his connection to the Unseen. He's drawing their power into himself, but if we break that link, the balance will be restored."

Vivian swallowed hard. "How do we do that?"

The professor glanced at him, and for the first time, Vivian saw a flicker of uncertainty in his eyes. "You're going to have to use the Quantum Spark, Vivian. But this time, you won't be creating something—you'll be unraveling it."

Vivian's heart skipped a beat. He had used the Quantum Spark to create, to shape reality, but this was something entirely different. He would be tampering with something far more dangerous—something that could spiral out of control if he wasn't careful.

But there was no time to hesitate. The Unseen were gathering, their forms growing more solid, more threatening, and the figure's power was increasing with every second.

Vivian gripped the Quantum Spark tightly, feeling its familiar pulse of energy in his hand. He closed his eyes, focusing on the figure, on the strange, shimmering energy that surrounded him. The air vibrated with potential, with the raw, chaotic power of the Unseen, and for a moment, Vivian felt as if he were standing on the edge of a precipice, staring into the infinite possibilities of the multiverse.

And then, with a deep breath, he reached out with his mind.

He could feel the threads of reality around him, the delicate weave of the multiverse that held everything together. The figure's connection to the Unseen was like a knot in that weave, pulling the threads tight, threatening to unravel everything. Vivian focused on that knot, imagining it loosening, unraveling.

At first, nothing happened. But then, slowly, he felt the knot begin to give way. The energy around the figure flickered, and the Unseen creatures hesitated, their forms wavering.

The figure's head snapped toward him, his eyes glowing with anger. "What are you doing?"

Vivian didn't answer. He focused harder, pulling at the threads of reality, willing the connection to break. The energy around the figure pulsed violently, and for a moment, the entire world seemed to shudder.

And then, with a final surge of power, the connection snapped.

The figure let out a scream, and the Unseen creatures dissolved into mist, their forms scattering into the air. The shimmering energy around the figure flickered and died, and he collapsed to the ground, his dark robes falling limp around him.

Vivian let out a shaky breath, his entire body trembling with the effort. The world around him seemed to settle, the strange hum fading into silence.

"You did it," the professor said softly, his voice filled with admiration. "You broke the connection."

Vivian stared at the fallen figure, his mind still reeling. He had felt the raw power of the multiverse, the infinite possibilities that lay just beyond the surface of reality. And for the first time, he understood just how fragile that balance was.

The professor placed a hand on his shoulder. "You've done well, Vivian. But remember—this was just a glimpse of the power that exists in the multiverse. There are forces out there far greater than this, and not all of them are as easily controlled."

Vivian nodded slowly, the weight of the experience settling in. He had come to the Nexus seeking adventure, but now he realized that the journey he was on was far more dangerous—and far more important—than he had ever imagined.

And somewhere, deep within the multiverse, the Unseen were still waiting.

Chapter 9: The Shadow of Chaos

The silence that followed the collapse of the Unseen felt heavy, as if the very air around Vivian had thickened with tension. The ground beneath him still pulsed faintly with the remnants of the strange energy that had stirred the creatures. The robed figure lay motionless in the distance, his connection to the Unseen severed, but the sense of unease lingered.

Professor Arcturus stared at the fallen figure, his brow furrowed. "Something is still wrong," he murmured.

Vivian felt it too. The knot of tension that had formed in his chest since the battle with the Unseen refused to loosen. Despite their victory, it was as if the Nexus itself was holding its breath, waiting for something to happen.

"What do you mean?" Vivian asked, his voice shaky.

The professor turned to him, his expression grave. "The Unseen are creatures of potential, of untapped possibility. When they are disturbed, the ripple effect spreads through the multiverse. This disturbance... it hasn't fully settled. In fact, I fear it has only just begun."

As the professor spoke, a low rumble echoed through the air. The ground beneath them trembled, and above, the sky—normally a tranquil swirl of iridescent colors—began to darken. Strange shapes flickered in the distance, like shadows moving within the very fabric of the sky itself.

Suddenly, the air was split by a sharp, piercing sound—like glass shattering. Vivian spun around, his heart racing, and saw it: a crack, a jagged tear in the very space around them. It hovered in the air, a swirling vortex of darkness that seemed to stretch endlessly into the void. Tendrils of shadowy energy began to spill from the crack, coiling and writhing as they reached out, searching for something to latch onto.

"What is that?" Vivian gasped, taking a step back.

"The Shadow of Chaos," the professor said grimly. "A force that emerges when the balance of reality is thrown into disarray. It feeds on instability, on the unraveling of possibility. If we don't stop it, it will consume everything in its path—entire dimensions could be swallowed by the chaos."

Vivian's pulse quickened. He had already witnessed the dangers of manipulating the multiverse, but this was something far worse. The tear in reality was growing, spreading, and the shadows that spilled from it seemed to move with purpose, as though they were alive.

"We have to close it," the professor said urgently, pulling out a small, handheld device that emitted a soft blue glow. "This crack is a direct result of the disruption caused by the Unseen. It's drawing energy from the multiverse, expanding with every passing moment."

"How do we stop it?" Vivian asked, his voice trembling.

"The same way you broke the connection with the Unseen," the professor said. "But this time, it will be much more dangerous. The Shadow of Chaos is not just a force—it's a living entity. It will resist your efforts to close the rift. You'll need to use the Quantum Spark to stabilize the tear, but be prepared for a fight."

Vivian swallowed hard, feeling the weight of the Quantum Spark in his hand. He had learned how to manipulate reality, how to create and undo, but this was something entirely different. The chaos that spilled from the crack wasn't just a tear in space—it was a hungry, sentient force that sought to devour everything in its path.

The shadows writhed around them, growing thicker, and Vivian felt a chill run down his spine as one of the tendrils reached out, brushing against his arm. It felt cold—unnaturally cold, like the touch of something that didn't belong in this world.

"Stay focused," the professor urged, stepping forward and activating the device in his hand. A faint hum filled the air as the device emitted a pulse of energy, creating a barrier that pushed back the encroaching shadows. "I'll keep the chaos at bay while you work. Use the Quantum

Spark to close the tear. But remember—this is no ordinary rift. The chaos will fight back."

Vivian nodded, his heart pounding in his chest. He could feel the chaotic energy swirling around him, pressing in on all sides. The Quantum Spark pulsed faintly in his hand, and for a moment, he hesitated. Could he really do this? Could he stabilize something so powerful, so dangerous?

There was no time to question himself. The shadows were growing stronger, and the crack in reality was widening. If they didn't act fast, the entire Nexus—and possibly the multiverse itself—would be consumed by chaos.

Taking a deep breath, Vivian stepped toward the tear. He reached out with his mind, focusing on the Quantum Spark, willing its energy to flow into the rift. The familiar sensation of power surged through him, and he felt the Quantum Spark respond, its energy spreading out like threads, reaching toward the edges of the tear.

At first, the crack seemed to shrink slightly, its jagged edges pulling together. But then, with a sudden surge, the shadows recoiled and struck back. Vivian staggered as a wave of dark energy slammed into him, knocking him to the ground. The shadows hissed and writhed, lashing out at him with tendrils of pure chaos.

"You must hold your ground!" the professor shouted, his voice strained as he fought to maintain the barrier. "The Shadow of Chaos will try to overwhelm you, but you cannot let it take control. You're stronger than it. Remember that!"

Vivian gritted his teeth, forcing himself to his feet. The shadows swirled around him, their cold tendrils reaching for his mind, his thoughts, trying to pull him into the chaos. But he fought back, focusing all his energy on the Quantum Spark.

The power of the Spark flared brighter, and he felt the threads of reality begin to respond. He reached deeper, pulling on the fabric of the multiverse, trying to weave the tear back together. The shadows hissed and screamed, their presence pushing against his will, but Vivian refused to give in.

With every ounce of strength, he willed the rift to close, visualizing the jagged edges knitting back together. Slowly, the crack began to shrink again, the shadows retreating as the rift's chaotic energy lost its hold on reality.

But just as the tear was about to seal completely, the Shadow of Chaos made one final, desperate move. A massive tendril of dark energy shot out from the rift, lashing toward Vivian with a speed that left no time to react.

In a split second, the professor stepped between Vivian and the tendril. The dark energy struck him with a violent force, knocking him to the ground.

"Professor!" Vivian screamed, rushing to his side.

The professor lay still, his body surrounded by faint traces of the chaotic energy. His breathing was shallow, his face pale.

Vivian felt a wave of panic wash over him. The tear in reality was nearly closed, but the cost had been too high. He knelt beside the professor, his hands shaking.

"Don't—don't worry about me," the professor whispered, his voice weak. "Finish the job, Vivian. Close the tear. You have to."

Tears stung Vivian's eyes as he looked up at the rift. The shadows were growing fainter, but they were still there, clinging to the last remnants of chaos that remained in the crack. With a final surge of effort, Vivian extended his hand, channeling the last of the Quantum Spark's energy into the rift.

The crack shuddered, its jagged edges pulling together one last time before finally sealing shut. The shadows dissolved, leaving nothing but silence in their wake.

For a moment, the world stood still.

Vivian collapsed beside the professor, his body trembling with exhaustion. The tear was gone, but the professor lay unconscious, his body weakened by the chaotic energy that had struck him.

"Professor," Vivian whispered, his voice hoarse. "I—I'm so sorry."

The professor's eyes fluttered open, and he managed a faint smile. "You did it, Vivian. You saved the Nexus."

"But at what cost?" Vivian asked, his heart heavy.

The professor placed a hand on his shoulder. "This... this is the price of power. The balance between creation and chaos is fragile. You've learned that now. But you've also learned that even in the face of destruction, you have the strength to protect what matters."

Vivian swallowed hard, his mind racing. He had saved the Nexus, but the professor's words echoed in his ears. The balance was fragile—too fragile. And the Shadow of Chaos had shown him just how easily things could spiral out of control.

As they sat together in the aftermath of the battle, Vivian felt a new sense of responsibility settle over him. He had come to the Nexus searching for adventure, but now he realized that the path he had chosen was far more dangerous than he had ever imagined.

The multiverse was vast and filled with wonders, but it was also filled with shadows—chaos waiting to tear it apart.

And somehow, Vivian knew that this wouldn't be the last time he would face it.

Chapter 10: The Ripple of Time

Days had passed since the battle with the Shadow of Chaos, but the experience lingered with Vivian like a shadow that clung to his thoughts. The Nexus seemed to have returned to its usual balance, but Vivian knew better. He could feel the subtle tension in the air, like the entire city was holding its breath, waiting for something to shift.

Professor Arcturus had recovered from the chaos-induced attack, though he still moved with a deliberate slowness, as if his body hadn't fully shaken off the effects of the chaotic energy. Despite his weakened state, he continued to teach Vivian with an urgency that hadn't been there before, as though he knew they had little time.

"Reality is more delicate than you realize," the professor had told Vivian one afternoon, his voice filled with quiet intensity. "What you did to close the rift was necessary, but it has left a mark. Chaos leaves ripples, and we are beginning to feel their effects."

That was how Vivian found himself standing on the outskirts of the Nexus once again, staring into the endless expanse of the multiverse. But this time, he wasn't here to close a rift. He was here to explore one.

The disturbance created by the Shadow of Chaos hadn't vanished completely. It had sent waves through the fabric of reality, causing subtle shifts in certain dimensions—worlds where time had warped, bending in on itself. The professor had sensed one such ripple nearby, a world where the flow of time was no longer linear, where past, present, and future collided in strange and unpredictable ways.

"Are you ready?" Professor Arcturus asked, standing beside him. His eyes were sharper now, despite his weakened appearance. He held a small, spherical device in his hand—something he called a Temporal Anchor, designed to stabilize them in a world where time was out of joint.

Vivian nodded, feeling the weight of the Quantum Spark in his hand. He had learned much since his first day in the Nexus, but he knew this would be one of his greatest challenges yet. Time was fragile, and meddling with it could have unforeseen consequences.

Together, they stepped forward, into the shimmering portal that led to the unstable dimension. The air shimmered as they passed through, and for a brief moment, Vivian felt like he was falling—tumbling through a void where time had no meaning.

And then, they emerged.

The world around them was both familiar and strange. They stood in the middle of a sprawling city, but the buildings were twisted, their structures blending ancient stonework with futuristic glass towers that shimmered like water. People moved through the streets, but they flickered in and out of existence, some moving with unnatural speed while others seemed frozen in place, their expressions blank and unaware.

"This is it," the professor said, glancing around. "A world where time has lost its flow. Moments from the past, present, and future are overlapping, creating temporal anomalies. We must be careful. The smallest action here could ripple across the timeline."

Vivian's heart raced as he took in the strange sights around him. He watched as a horse-drawn carriage flickered into existence beside a hovering car, the two vehicles passing through one another as though they were made of mist. In the distance, a massive clock tower stood, its hands spinning wildly in all directions, as if time itself were in chaos.

"What caused this?" Vivian asked, his voice barely above a whisper.

The professor's expression was grim. "The disturbance we encountered—the Shadow of Chaos—it's left scars on the multiverse. Time is one of the most fragile elements of reality, and once it's disrupted, the effects can spread like cracks through glass."

Vivian swallowed hard. He had already seen the consequences of disrupting reality, but this—this was something else entirely. The idea that time itself could be fractured, that entire moments could collide and bleed into one another, made his head spin.

"Can we fix it?" Vivian asked, his voice filled with uncertainty.

The professor nodded slowly. "Yes, but it will be difficult. We need to locate the central point where the timeline is unraveling. Once we find it, we can use the Temporal Anchor to stabilize the flow of time and prevent further anomalies from spreading."

They moved through the city cautiously, watching as the strange, flickering figures moved past them. Vivian saw people dressed in old-fashioned clothing, their movements jerky and unnatural, mingling with others who appeared to be from far into the future, their bodies augmented with strange, glowing technology. Time, it seemed, had lost all meaning here.

As they walked, the professor explained more about the nature of time in the multiverse. "Time is not a straight line, as many imagine it to be," he said. "It's more like a river—flowing, branching, sometimes looping back on itself. In some dimensions, time flows differently, more like a spiral or a web. But here, it's completely unraveled."

Vivian nodded, trying to make sense of it all. He had never given much thought to the nature of time before—back home, it had always seemed like something simple and unchanging. But now, in this fractured world, he realized just how complex and fragile time truly was.

As they reached the center of the city, the anomalies grew more pronounced. Entire buildings flickered in and out of existence, some collapsing into ruins before rebuilding themselves in an instant. In the distance, Vivian saw a towering monument—an ancient statue—appear for a brief moment before vanishing, replaced by a sleek, futuristic skyscraper.

"We're close," the professor said, his voice tense. "I can feel it."

Suddenly, a sharp crackling sound filled the air, and Vivian felt a jolt of energy race through him. He spun around and saw it—a tear in the fabric of time, much like the one they had seen in the Nexus. But this tear wasn't just spilling shadows—it was spilling *moments*.

From the tear, events from the past, present, and future poured out, overlapping and colliding in a chaotic swirl. Vivian watched in horror as a battle from centuries ago played out beside a scene of peaceful, futuristic negotiations. Soldiers in ancient armor clashed with diplomats wearing glowing robes, their movements jerky and unnatural as they flickered in and out of existence.

"We have to close it," the professor said urgently. "But this tear is different from the last one. It's not just chaos—it's time itself unraveling. We'll need to carefully weave the threads of time back together, or we risk destroying this entire dimension."

Vivian's heart pounded in his chest. This was far beyond anything he had ever done. But there was no turning back now. He gripped the Quantum Spark tightly, feeling its energy pulse in his hand.

The professor handed him the Temporal Anchor, its surface glowing softly. "I'll stabilize the tear," he said, "but you'll need to use the Quantum Spark to guide the flow of time, to pull the moments back into place."

Vivian nodded, his mind racing. He had learned how to create and unravel reality, but this—this was a new level of complexity. He closed his eyes, focusing on the tear, on the swirling chaos of moments pouring from it.

With a deep breath, he reached out with his mind, connecting with the Quantum Spark. He could feel the threads of time—frayed, tangled, and knotted—stretching out before him. It was like trying to grasp the strands of a spider's web, each thread delicate and interconnected.

Slowly, carefully, he began to pull on the threads, guiding them back into place. The past, present, and future swirled around him, and he felt the weight of each moment as it passed through his mind. He saw flashes of battles long forgotten, glimpses of worlds that had yet to be born, and echoes of decisions that would shape entire realities.

But as he worked, the tear fought back. The chaotic energy surged, and the threads of time slipped through his grasp, twisting and unraveling faster than he could control them.

"You can do this!" the professor called out, his voice strained as he struggled to maintain the stabilizing field around the tear. "Stay focused!"

Vivian gritted his teeth, his mind racing as he tried to regain control. He could feel the pull of the past, the weight of the future, pressing down on him. The moments he was trying to weave together were like living things, fighting against him, trying to break free.

But then, in the chaos, he saw it—a single, golden thread. It was faint, almost imperceptible, but it pulsed with a steady rhythm, untouched by the swirling storm around it.

The *true* timeline.

Vivian reached for it, focusing all his energy on that single thread. As his mind connected with it, the other threads began to fall into place, drawn to the golden thread like iron filings to a magnet. The past, present, and future began to align, the chaos settling into order.

The tear shuddered, and with a final pulse of energy, it snapped shut.

For a moment, the world stood still.

The chaotic moments that had spilled from the tear faded, and the city around them began to stabilize. The buildings, the people, the very air itself seemed to breathe a sigh of relief as time returned to its proper flow.

Vivian let out a shaky breath, his entire body trembling with exhaustion. He had done it—he had restored the flow of time. But the effort had drained him, both mentally and physically.

The professor stepped forward, placing a hand on his shoulder. "You've done well, Vivian. Better than I could have hoped."

Vivian nodded, still trying to catch his breath. "But what caused this? Was it the Shadow of Chaos?"

The professor's expression darkened. "Partly. But there's something else at play here—something deeper. The multiverse is reacting to the disturbances we've seen. Forces that have been dormant for centuries are beginning to stir."

Vivian's heart sank. He had thought that closing the tear would be the end of it, but now he realized that this was only the beginning. The multiverse was fragile, and the events he had been part of were rippling across countless dimensions, affecting realities in ways he couldn't yet understand.

As they stood together in the now-stable city, Vivian felt a new sense of resolve. He had come to the Nexus searching for adventure, but now he knew that his journey was far more important than he had ever imagined. There were forces at work that could unravel the very fabric of the multiverse, and it was up to him—and Professor Arcturus—to stop them.

But as they prepared to return to the Nexus, Vivian couldn't shake the feeling that the true battle was yet to come.

Chapter 11: The Fractured Path

The Nexus had never felt so quiet. After restoring the fractured timeline in the chaotic dimension, Vivian returned to the city with a sense of weariness, but also a growing sense of foreboding. The streets hummed with their usual energy, yet something felt...off. As though the Nexus itself was holding its breath, waiting for something to break.

Professor Arcturus hadn't said much since they returned, his face lined with worry. The aftermath of their encounter with the tear in time weighed heavily on both of them. The professor had always spoken of balance, of how the multiverse was delicate and could unravel with even the smallest disruption. But now, it seemed like the disruptions were becoming more frequent—more dangerous.

Vivian could feel the weight of it all pressing down on him. He had learned so much since he arrived, but the more he discovered about the Nexus and the multiverse, the more uncertain he felt about the path ahead.

"Come with me," Professor Arcturus said suddenly, breaking the silence. He stood in the doorway of his study, his eyes sharp with determination.

Vivian rose to his feet, feeling the tension in the air as he followed the professor. They moved through the halls of the Nexus Institute in silence, passing shimmering holograms and glowing machines. Every step felt like it was leading to something inevitable.

They stopped before a door that Vivian had never seen before. It was carved from dark wood, with strange runes etched into its surface. The air around it pulsed faintly, like a heartbeat.

"This is the Hall of Reflections," the professor said quietly. "A place where the boundaries between realities are thin. Here, you can glimpse into parallel dimensions—see the paths not taken."

Vivian's heart skipped a beat. He had heard of parallel worlds, of alternate versions of reality where choices made or not made shaped different lives, different outcomes. But he had never imagined being able to see them—let alone interact with them.

The professor placed a hand on the door, and it creaked open, revealing a vast, empty chamber. At its center was a shimmering pool of liquid light, swirling with colors that Vivian couldn't name. The pool seemed to stretch into infinity, its surface rippling as though it were alive.

"I brought you here for a reason," the professor said, his voice low. "What we encountered in the fractured timeline was only the beginning. The multiverse is reacting to something...something much larger than we've faced before. And I believe you're at the center of it."

Vivian's eyes widened. "Me? How could I be causing this?"

The professor turned to face him, his expression serious. "The Quantum Spark is a rare and powerful artifact, but it's not just a tool for creation. It connects you to the very fabric of the multiverse, allowing you to shape reality—but also to disrupt it. Every choice you make, every action you take, ripples across dimensions."

Vivian felt a chill run down his spine. He had known the Spark was powerful, but he hadn't realized just how far-reaching its effects could be.

"The Hall of Reflections will show you what might have been," the professor continued. "The choices you didn't make, the paths you didn't take. And somewhere in those reflections, I believe we'll find the answer to why the multiverse is unraveling."

Vivian swallowed hard, his gaze locked on the swirling pool. The idea of seeing alternate versions of himself, of his life, was both thrilling and terrifying. But if it would help him understand what was happening, he knew he had no choice.

He stepped forward, his heart pounding in his chest as he knelt beside the pool. The liquid light rippled, casting strange shadows on the walls. Slowly, Vivian reached out with his mind, using the Quantum Spark to connect with the pool's energy.

The moment he made contact, the world around him shifted.

He was no longer in the Hall of Reflections. Instead, he found himself standing in a vast, mirrored landscape, stretching out as far as he could see. Each reflection showed a different version of him—some almost identical, others wildly different. In one, he was still back home, living a mundane life without adventure. In another, he was older, wiser, his body cloaked in shimmering energy as he wielded the full power of the Quantum Spark. And in yet another, he stood at the heart of a ruined Nexus, its once-glowing towers crumbled to dust.

Vivian's breath caught in his throat. The reflections were more than just possibilities—they were real, living versions of himself, each one shaped by the choices he had made or failed to make.

As he stepped closer to one of the mirrors, his reflection rippled, and the image changed. He saw himself standing on a battlefield, surrounded by chaos. In this world, the Nexus had fallen, and the multiverse was in ruins. His eyes glowed with power, but his face was hard, cold. He wore a suit of dark armor, and in his hand, he held a blade of pure energy, crackling with chaotic force.

"This...this can't be real," Vivian whispered, stepping back from the mirror.

But before he could turn away, the reflection moved.

Vivian froze as the reflection stepped out of the mirror, becoming solid, real. It was him—but not him. This version of Vivian was taller, older, his face etched with scars. His eyes glowed with the same strange energy that had spilled from the tear in time, and his presence radiated a cold, terrifying power.

"Well, well," the other Vivian said, his voice smooth but laced with menace. "So, this is the path you've taken. The path of hesitation, of weakness."

Vivian's heart raced as he faced his alternate self. "What are you?"

The other Vivian smirked. "I'm you. Or at least, the version of you that didn't shy away from the truth. I embraced the full power of the

Quantum Spark, and in doing so, I gained control of the multiverse. But it came at a cost—a cost you're too afraid to pay."

Vivian shook his head, backing away. "No, that's not what I want. I don't want to control anything."

"That's the difference between us," the other Vivian said, stepping closer. "You're still clinging to the idea that you can fix things, that you can maintain balance. But the multiverse isn't about balance—it's about power. And the sooner you realize that, the sooner you'll understand that this is the only path."

Vivian felt a surge of fear. This version of him had embraced the darkness, the chaos, and it had consumed him. He had become a twisted reflection of everything Vivian had feared.

"I won't become you," Vivian said, his voice steady despite the fear coursing through him. "I won't let the power control me."

The other Vivian's eyes narrowed. "Then you're a fool."

Without warning, the dark Vivian raised his hand, and a surge of chaotic energy shot toward Vivian, crackling with raw power. Vivian barely had time to react. He raised the Quantum Spark, channeling its energy to form a shield around him. The blast struck the shield, sending ripples of force through the air, but the Spark held firm.

The other Vivian smiled darkly. "You're stronger than I expected. But strength won't save you. The multiverse is already unraveling, and unless you're willing to embrace the chaos, you'll be consumed by it."

Vivian gritted his teeth, feeling the weight of the Quantum Spark in his hand. He had faced chaos before, but this—this was different. This was personal.

The dark Vivian raised his hand again, but before he could strike, Professor Arcturus appeared, stepping between them.

"Enough!" the professor shouted, his voice filled with authority. "You are nothing but a reflection—a possibility. And your path is not the one that will decide the fate of the multiverse."

The dark Vivian's eyes flickered with anger, but he didn't attack. Instead, he lowered his hand, his smirk returning. "Perhaps. But your apprentice will soon learn that power is not something that can be controlled forever. One way or another, he will become me."

With a final, mocking glance, the dark Vivian faded, dissolving back into the mirror from which he had emerged.

For a long moment, the room was silent. Vivian stood frozen, his heart racing, his mind spinning with the implications of what he had just seen.

Professor Arcturus placed a hand on his shoulder. "You did well to resist him. But now you see the danger that lies ahead. The power of the Quantum Spark can lead you down many paths—some darker than others. The choices you make from here on will determine not only your fate but the fate of the multiverse."

Vivian nodded slowly, still shaken by the encounter. "I never thought... I never realized how much power could change me."

The professor's expression softened. "That's why we must tread carefully. You are at a crossroads, Vivian. You've seen what could happen if you lose control, if you let the power consume you. But you've also seen the strength within you—the strength to choose a different path."

Vivian took a deep breath, his resolve hardening. He had come to the Nexus searching for adventure, for something more than the ordinary life he had known. But now, he understood the true cost of the power he wielded.

"I won't let it control me," Vivian said quietly. "I won't become him."

The professor smiled. "Good. Then we still have a chance."

As they left the Hall of Reflections, Vivian felt a new sense of purpose growing within him. He had seen the path he could take—the path of chaos, of darkness. But he had also seen the strength it took to resist it.

The multiverse was vast, filled with infinite possibilities, and the choices he made would ripple across countless realities. But now, he knew that he didn't have to face those choices alone.

With Professor Arcturus by his side, Vivian was ready to face whatever came next.

Chapter 12: The Unraveling Begins

The Hall of Reflections loomed behind them as Vivian and Professor Arcturus walked in silence through the streets of the Nexus. The encounter with his fractured self had left Vivian shaken to his core. The dark version of himself had been more than a reflection—it had been a warning. But the sense of looming danger hadn't left him. If anything, it had only grown stronger.

For days after the encounter, strange things began happening around the Nexus. Dimensional rifts, much smaller than the one they had faced before, flickered at the edges of reality. Some were brief—a street corner bending in on itself before snapping back into place—but others lingered, disrupting the flow of time or causing buildings to phase in and out of existence.

It was as though the very threads of reality were fraying, unweaving in subtle but dangerous ways.

Vivian spent long hours with the professor, trying to stabilize the anomalies, using the Quantum Spark to sew the fabric of reality back together. But with each tear they closed, another seemed to open elsewhere, as though something—*someone*—was actively pulling at the edges of the multiverse.

"It's not just natural chaos," Professor Arcturus said one evening, his brow furrowed as they stood before a new rift. "These disruptions... they're targeted. Someone or something is destabilizing the Nexus on purpose."

Vivian's pulse quickened. He had suspected as much, but hearing it confirmed sent a chill down his spine. "But why? What do they want?"

"Power," the professor replied grimly. "Control over the multiverse. There are forces that would seek to unravel the balance we've worked so hard to maintain. The Quantum Spark gives you a glimpse of that power, but there are beings out there who would stop at nothing to control it completely."

Vivian clenched his fists, his grip tightening around the Quantum Spark. He had seen firsthand what that power could do—how it could corrupt and twist even the most well-meaning intentions. And now, it seemed, those forces were gathering, threatening to undo everything.

As they worked to close another tear, the world around them suddenly shifted. A low rumble filled the air, and the ground trembled beneath their feet. Vivian stumbled, looking up to see the sky darkening, the familiar glow of the Nexus fading into an eerie twilight.

A voice echoed through the air, cold and calculating, cutting through the rumble of the shifting reality. "So, the apprentice steps into the game at last."

Vivian spun around, his heart pounding, and saw a figure standing at the edge of the rift they had just sealed. The figure wore a dark, flowing cloak, their face hidden beneath a hood, but the aura of power that radiated from them was unmistakable. They moved with a grace that defied the chaos around them, as though they were untouched by the fraying edges of reality.

The professor's face darkened as he stepped forward. "Who are you?"

The figure let out a low chuckle, the sound sending a shiver down Vivian's spine. "Who am I?" the figure repeated, their voice soft but menacing. "I am the one who sees beyond the limits of this fragile reality. I am the hand that guides the unraveling of the multiverse. And soon, I will be its master."

Vivian's heart raced. This was no ordinary threat—this was the force behind the disruptions, the one pulling the strings.

"You're causing the rifts," Vivian said, his voice shaking with a mixture of fear and anger. "You're trying to destroy the Nexus."

"Destroy it?" the figure mused, taking a step closer. "No, child. I'm liberating it. The Nexus is a prison, a place where the natural flow of chaos is shackled by the chains of order. I seek to free it—to let the multiverse return to its true state of potential, unbound by the restrictions of balance."

The professor's expression hardened. "You're meddling with forces you don't understand. The Nexus holds the multiverse together. Without it, reality would collapse into chaos."

"Chaos is not the enemy," the figure countered, their voice growing more intense. "It is the foundation of all creation. You have spent too long trying to control it, but you cannot cage the infinite. I will return the multiverse to its natural state, and in doing so, I will become its ruler."

Vivian felt a surge of defiance rise within him. He had seen the damage that unchecked chaos could cause. He had seen the darkness that lay at the heart of power without responsibility. And he knew that the figure standing before them sought nothing less than absolute domination over reality itself.

"You're wrong," Vivian said, stepping forward, his voice filled with determination. "Chaos without control leads to destruction. You don't want to free the multiverse—you want to control it. But I won't let you."

The figure's hood tilted slightly, as though they were studying him. "Ah, the apprentice speaks with conviction. But conviction alone will not save you. The power you wield, the Quantum Spark—it connects you to the multiverse, yes, but it also binds you. It limits you. I, on the other hand, am not bound by such restrictions."

With a swift, fluid motion, the figure raised their hand, and the rift that they had just closed ripped open once more, larger and more unstable than before. Tendrils of dark energy spilled from it, coiling through the air like serpents, reaching toward Vivian and the professor.

Vivian reacted instinctively, raising the Quantum Spark and forming a barrier around them. The dark energy slammed into the shield, sending ripples of force through the air, but the Spark held firm.

"You cannot hold me back forever," the figure said, their voice laced with amusement. "The multiverse is already unraveling. Soon, the Nexus will fall, and with it, the balance you so desperately cling to."

The professor's eyes narrowed, his voice sharp with authority. "You underestimate the strength of those who protect the Nexus. We will stop you."

The figure let out a low, mocking laugh. "You cannot stop what has already begun. The Nexus was built on the illusion of control, but that control is slipping. The chaos will consume you all, and when it does, I will rise from the ashes."

Vivian's heart pounded as the tendrils of dark energy continued to press against the barrier. He could feel the weight of the figure's power, the sheer force of their will pressing down on him. But he refused to give in.

"We need to close the rift," Vivian said through gritted teeth, struggling to maintain the barrier. "Before it spreads."

The professor nodded, his expression grim. "Focus on the rift. I'll deal with our...guest."

With a flick of his wrist, the professor summoned a series of glowing runes in the air, each one crackling with energy. The runes spun in a tight circle around the figure, forming a barrier of their own.

The figure let out a soft chuckle. "You think your spells can hold me? How quaint."

But as the figure moved to step forward, the runes flared brightly, forcing them to halt. The professor's magic was strong—strong enough to contain even a being as powerful as this. But Vivian knew it wouldn't last long.

He turned his focus back to the rift, the Quantum Spark pulsing in his hand. The tear in reality was larger now, spilling raw, chaotic energy into the world. It writhed and twisted like a living thing, resisting his attempts to close it.

With every ounce of focus, Vivian reached out with his mind, weaving the frayed edges of reality back together. He could feel the resistance of the chaos, but he pushed through, pulling the threads tight, sealing the tear inch by inch.

The figure, still trapped within the professor's runes, watched with interest. "You're stronger than I expected, apprentice," they said, their voice smooth and calm. "But you're only delaying the inevitable. The multiverse cannot be contained."

Vivian gritted his teeth, ignoring the taunts. He focused all his energy on the rift, channeling the power of the Quantum Spark into it. Slowly, the tear began to shrink, the chaotic energy retreating as the edges of reality knit themselves back together.

And then, with a final surge of power, the rift snapped shut.

Vivian staggered back, his body trembling with exhaustion. The weight of the effort had drained him, but the rift was sealed. The immediate threat had passed.

But the figure was still there, watching him with a strange intensity.

"You may have won this battle," they said softly, their voice barely above a whisper. "But the war is far from over. The Nexus is unraveling, and there is nothing you can do to stop it."

With a flick of their hand, the runes surrounding the figure dissolved, and they began to fade from view, their form dissolving into the shadows.

"Remember this, apprentice," the figure said, their voice echoing in the air. "The multiverse is not yours to control. It will bend to the will of those strong enough to shape it. And soon, you will see the truth."

And with that, the figure vanished, leaving only silence in their wake.

Vivian stood frozen, his mind racing. He had won—at least, for now. But the figure's words lingered, haunting him. The multiverse was unraveling, and somewhere out there, a force far greater than he had ever imagined was working to tear it apart.

Professor Arcturus placed a hand on his shoulder, his voice quiet but steady. "This is just the beginning, Vivian. The true threat is still out there. And we must be ready to face it."

Vivian nodded, his resolve hardening. He had come to the Nexus seeking adventure, but now he understood the full weight of the responsibility that had been placed on him. The multiverse was fragile, and its fate rested in his hands.

But as they walked back through the darkened streets of the Nexus, Vivian couldn't shake the feeling that the figure's words had held a terrible truth.

The unraveling had begun.

Chapter 13: The Gathering Storm

The streets of the Nexus were quieter than usual, the usual hum of energy and life dimmed by an undercurrent of fear. Word had spread of the growing instability—people sensed that something was wrong, even if they couldn't put it into words. The once-vibrant city of impossible science and magic now felt like a ticking clock, counting down to an unknown catastrophe.

Vivian and Professor Arcturus had retreated to the Nexus Institute, poring over scrolls of ancient texts and holographic projections of multiverse maps. The mysterious figure they had encountered weighed heavily on their minds. Whoever—or whatever—they were, they had the power to open rifts with ease and command chaos like a force of nature.

"It doesn't add up," Vivian said, his voice low as he studied the glowing holograms. "How can someone control the rifts like that? They're connected to the multiverse, but this figure seemed to manipulate them effortlessly."

The professor, his expression as grim as ever, leaned back in his chair. "That's what we need to understand. The Quantum Spark allows you to connect with the multiverse, to influence its fabric, but even that has limits. For someone to control rifts on this scale, they would need access to a power beyond the Nexus itself."

Vivian frowned, staring at the swirling projections of the multiverse. "But what kind of power could do that? And how are they connected to the rifts?"

Professor Arcturus tapped a glowing orb on the table, and the holographic map zoomed in on several dimensions surrounding the Nexus. "There are ancient forces at work here. Forces that existed long before the Nexus was created. Long before we understood the multiverse as we do now."

Vivian's heart quickened. "What kind of forces?"

The professor hesitated for a moment before answering, his voice soft but heavy with significance. "The Elders of the Multiverse. Beings of immense power, some of whom are said to have shaped the early fabric of reality itself. They existed in the dark spaces between dimensions, long before the Nexus brought balance to the multiverse."

Vivian stared at him in disbelief. "I thought they were just myths."

"Most believe they are," the professor said, his eyes narrowing. "But if they are real, and if this figure has somehow tapped into their power, then we may be dealing with something far more dangerous than we ever imagined."

Vivian felt a chill creep up his spine. The idea that beings as old as the multiverse itself could be involved was overwhelming. If the Elders were real, and if the figure had their power at his disposal, then the balance of the entire multiverse could be at stake.

Before he could voice his thoughts, a soft chime echoed through the room. The professor glanced up, his eyes sharp. "We have a visitor."

Vivian turned to see a shimmering light appear in the center of the room. The air rippled, and a figure stepped through—a tall woman clad in armor made of glowing silver, her long hair cascading like molten metal. Her eyes gleamed with an inner light, and her presence seemed to fill the room with an aura of authority.

"Professor Arcturus," she said, her voice smooth but commanding. "I bring urgent news."

The professor rose to his feet, bowing slightly. "Lady Taryn. It's been a long time."

Vivian's eyes widened. He had heard of Lady Taryn before—one of the legendary Guardians of the Nexus, warriors sworn to protect the balance of the multiverse. They were rarely seen, spending most of their time at the edges of reality, keeping watch over the fragile threads that held the dimensions together.

Lady Taryn turned her gaze to Vivian, studying him for a moment before speaking. "This must be your apprentice."

Vivian straightened, feeling a mix of awe and nervousness under her piercing gaze. "Yes, I'm Vivian."

The Guardian nodded, then turned back to the professor. "We've detected multiple disruptions across several key dimensions. The rifts are spreading, faster than we anticipated. Whatever force is behind this has gained significant control over the chaos."

"We've encountered the one responsible," the professor said, his voice grim. "A figure cloaked in shadow, wielding the power to open and control rifts. They claimed they wanted to 'free' the multiverse from balance."

Lady Taryn's expression hardened. "I feared as much. The Council of Guardians has been monitoring a surge in chaotic energy throughout the multiverse. We believe this figure may be working in conjunction with one of the ancient forces—the Elders."

Vivian felt his breath catch. "So the Elders are real?"

"They are more than real," Lady Taryn said, her eyes narrowing. "And if one of them has returned, we are all in grave danger. The Elders thrive on chaos, and they have no interest in preserving balance. To them, the multiverse is nothing more than a canvas for destruction and rebirth. If this figure has allied with them, they may be trying to tear down the Nexus itself."

The weight of her words settled over the room like a storm cloud. Vivian exchanged a glance with the professor. The situation was worse than they had imagined.

"Is there a way to stop them?" Vivian asked, his voice tight with urgency.

Lady Taryn's expression softened slightly. "There is. But it will not be easy. We must track down the source of the chaos, the central point from which the rifts are being controlled. If we can sever the connection between this figure and the Elders, we may be able to restore balance."

The professor nodded, his face set with determination. "Then we'll need to move quickly. The rifts are spreading too fast. If we don't act soon, they could destabilize entire dimensions."

Lady Taryn's gaze sharpened. "There is one more thing you should know. The Guardians have detected a significant disturbance within a critical dimension—one that connects directly to the Nexus. We believe this is where the figure is hiding, using the chaos from that dimension to spread the rifts across the multiverse."

Vivian's heart raced. "Which dimension?"

Lady Taryn turned to him, her expression grave. "The dimension you came from, Vivian. Your home world."

Vivian's blood ran cold. His mind raced with the implications. The dimension he had left behind, the world he had grown up in—was now at the heart of the chaos spreading across the multiverse.

"We need to go there immediately," the professor said, his voice urgent. "If the figure is hiding there, we can't waste any more time."

Lady Taryn nodded. "I've already arranged for a portal. But be warned—this will not be like the other disruptions you've faced. The chaos has taken deep root in that dimension. Time and reality may not behave as they should."

Vivian felt a knot of fear tighten in his chest. The idea of returning to his world, to the place he had left behind in search of adventure, filled him with both dread and a strange sense of responsibility. If his home world was at the center of the chaos, then it was up to him to help stop it.

"I'm ready," he said, his voice steady despite the fear swirling inside him. "We have to stop this."

The professor placed a hand on his shoulder, his gaze firm. "You've come a long way, Vivian. But this will be your greatest challenge yet. Stay focused. Trust in your training. We'll face whatever comes together."

Vivian nodded, his resolve hardening. He had faced chaos before, but this was different. This was personal.

Lady Taryn led them to the portal room, where a shimmering gate of light stood ready. Beyond it, Vivian could see the faint outlines of his home world—the familiar skyline of the city he had once known, now warped by the presence of the rifts.

As they stepped through the portal, Vivian felt the weight of the Quantum Spark in his hand, its energy pulsing faintly. The storm was gathering, and the multiverse was unraveling faster than ever.

But this time, he wouldn't run from it.

He would face it head-on.

Chapter 14: Return to a Broken World

The portal shimmered, casting a soft glow over the room as Vivian, Professor Arcturus, and Lady Taryn stood at its threshold. Beyond the swirling gate of light, the familiar outline of Vivian's home dimension beckoned—yet it was anything but the world he had left behind. Distorted buildings leaned at impossible angles, the sky above flickered between shades of day and night, and faint rifts scarred the very fabric of reality, stretching across the skyline like jagged wounds.

Vivian's heart pounded in his chest as he took a step toward the portal, his breath catching in his throat. He hadn't been back since the day he had volunteered to step into the time machine, seeking escape from the monotony of his life. Now, he was returning not as a bored twelve-year-old, but as someone who had seen the vastness of the multiverse, and the terrible power that came with it.

But the sight of his world, fractured and broken, sent a pang of guilt through him. Had his departure, or something about his connection to the Quantum Spark, allowed the chaos to take root here?

"You're not alone in this, Vivian," Professor Arcturus said gently, placing a hand on his shoulder. "We'll face whatever is waiting for us together."

Lady Taryn stepped forward, her silver armor gleaming faintly in the light of the portal. "We must be cautious," she said. "The chaos here is deeply rooted. Reality will not behave as it should. Time, space—they will warp and bend. Stay close, and trust in the power of the Spark."

Vivian nodded, gripping the Quantum Spark tightly in his hand. The energy within it pulsed faintly, as though sensing the growing instability around them.

Taking a deep breath, he stepped through the portal.

The moment they crossed the threshold, the air changed. It felt heavier, thick with the strange, unnatural presence of chaos. The city streets that once felt so familiar now seemed alien, warped by the presence of rifts that shimmered and flickered with unstable energy. Time itself seemed fractured—one moment, the city was silent and still, and the next, it shifted, blurring with the echoes of both the past and the future.

Vivian stumbled slightly as his mind struggled to adjust to the strange sensations. His home city—the place he had known so well—was no longer recognizable. Shadows moved in the corners of his vision, as though fragments of different timelines were converging, overlapping in ways that defied all logic.

"This is worse than I thought," Lady Taryn muttered, scanning the streets with sharp eyes. "The rifts are spreading faster here. This dimension is on the brink of collapse."

Vivian felt his heart clench. He had imagined returning home to see the familiar faces and places he had left behind, but now, it seemed like those remnants were slipping away, dissolving into the chaos that was tearing this world apart.

As they moved deeper into the city, the streets became more distorted. Buildings shifted in and out of existence, flickering between the forms they once held and strange, impossible shapes. The ground beneath their feet rippled like water, and occasionally, they passed people—figures who seemed frozen in time, trapped in loops of their own memories, or walking in a haze as though they existed in multiple moments at once.

"Do they know what's happening?" Vivian asked quietly, watching as a man in a suit walked down the street only to vanish, reappearing moments later as his younger self, before fading again.

"They're caught between timelines," the professor explained. "The rifts have fractured their connection to the present. Some are experiencing the past, others the future. Time is broken here."

Vivian swallowed hard. He had never imagined chaos like this—time and space unraveling, lives reduced to echoes of what once was or might have been.

As they continued forward, the air grew colder, and the flickering of reality intensified. Vivian felt the Quantum Spark pulse in his hand, its energy responding to the instability around them.

Suddenly, Lady Taryn came to an abrupt stop, her eyes narrowing as she scanned the horizon. "Do you feel that?"

Vivian frowned, focusing on the subtle shift in the air. There was something there—something dark and powerful, lurking just beyond their senses.

Professor Arcturus nodded grimly. "We're getting close."

As they pressed forward, the streets became more twisted, the rifts more pronounced. Vivian could feel the pull of chaos growing stronger, like a weight pressing down on his chest. And then, they reached it—the heart of the disturbance.

It was a massive rift, larger than any they had seen before. It hovered in the air above a wide square in the city, its edges crackling with dark energy. The rift seemed to pulse, drawing in fragments of time and space, warping everything around it. The buildings near the rift had been twisted into grotesque shapes, and the ground beneath it rippled with waves of chaotic force.

And standing at the center of it all was the figure.

The same hooded figure from before, their dark cloak billowing in the shifting winds of the rift. But now, their presence felt even more overwhelming, their power radiating outward, distorting the very air around them.

Vivian's pulse quickened as he recognized the figure's silhouette. This was the force behind the chaos, the one who had claimed they would free the multiverse from balance.

"You've returned," the figure said, their voice carrying a sinister edge as they turned to face Vivian. "I knew you couldn't stay away for long."

"Stop this," Vivian said, stepping forward, his voice filled with determination. "You're destroying this world—you're tearing it apart."

The figure let out a low, amused chuckle. "I'm not destroying it. I'm liberating it. This world is already broken, caught in the chains of time and order. I'm simply releasing it from those bonds, allowing it to return to its true, chaotic nature."

Vivian's grip on the Quantum Spark tightened. "You're wrong. Chaos like this doesn't create freedom—it only leads to destruction."

The figure's eyes, glowing with an eerie light beneath the hood, narrowed. "You still cling to the illusion of control, apprentice. But you'll soon learn that control is a lie. The multiverse was never meant to be ordered. It was meant to be wild, untamed. And once this world falls, the Nexus will follow."

Vivian's heart raced as the figure raised their hand, and the rift pulsed, sending a wave of chaotic energy through the square. The ground shook violently, and the buildings around them began to crumble, their forms dissolving into swirling clouds of dust and light.

"Vivian, now!" Professor Arcturus shouted.

Without hesitation, Vivian raised the Quantum Spark, channeling its energy toward the rift. The Spark pulsed with power, and threads of light extended from it, reaching toward the edges of the tear in reality. But as soon as the threads made contact with the rift, the figure lashed out.

A tendril of dark energy shot from the rift, slamming into Vivian's shield. He staggered back, struggling to maintain control as the force of the attack sent ripples through his defenses.

"You cannot stop me," the figure hissed. "The rift is beyond your power now."

Vivian gritted his teeth, pushing back against the dark energy. He could feel the weight of the chaos pressing down on him, trying to overwhelm his connection to the Quantum Spark. But he refused to give in.

Beside him, Lady Taryn unleashed a wave of silver light, striking at the tendrils of chaos. Her sword gleamed as it cut through the swirling darkness, and for a brief moment, the pressure on Vivian's shield eased.

"You're not alone in this fight, Vivian," she said, her voice steady and fierce.

Vivian nodded, focusing all his energy on the rift. He could feel the Quantum Spark responding, its power growing as he drew from the threads of reality around him. Slowly, the rift began to shrink, the chaotic energy pulling inward as the Spark's light pushed against it.

But the figure was not finished.

With a sudden, violent motion, the figure unleashed a torrent of energy from the rift. The force of it slammed into Vivian, knocking him to the ground. His vision blurred as the world spun around him, the weight of the chaos crushing down on his mind.

For a moment, he felt as though he was falling—falling through the rift, into the heart of the chaos itself.

But then, through the storm of darkness, he heard a voice.

Focus, Vivian. You have the power to control this. You are connected to the Spark. Trust it.

It was Professor Arcturus.

Vivian clenched his fists, his mind latching onto the professor's words. The Quantum Spark pulsed in his hand, its energy flowing through him like a lifeline. He focused, drawing on everything he had learned—everything he had experienced since coming to the Nexus.

The darkness pressed in, but he pushed back.

With a surge of determination, Vivian rose to his feet, the Quantum Spark blazing with light. He reached out with his mind, grasping the edges of the rift, weaving the threads of time and space back together.

The rift resisted, its chaotic energy thrashing against him. But Vivian held firm. He could feel the Spark's power flowing through him, stronger than ever before. Slowly, the rift began to close, the dark energy pulling inward as the tear in reality sealed itself shut.

The figure let out a furious scream as the rift vanished, their form flickering in and out of existence as the chaos around them dissipated.

"You think this is over?" the figure hissed, their voice filled with venom. "This is only the beginning. The Nexus will fall. The multiverse will crumble. And you will see that chaos cannot be contained."

And with that, the figure dissolved into the air, disappearing into the shadows.

For a moment, the square was silent. The rift was gone, and the chaotic energy that had gripped the city began to fade. But the sense of foreboding lingered.

Vivian stood still, his body trembling with exhaustion, but his mind was sharper than ever.

This wasn't over.

The storm was still gathering.

And the true battle was yet to come.

Chapter 15: The Nexus Under Siege

The moment they stepped back through the portal into the Nexus, Vivian knew something had changed.

The air, once filled with the hum of magic and science in harmony, now crackled with an unnatural tension. The sky above the city was dark, not from nightfall, but from the swirling clouds of chaos that had begun to gather. Faint, flickering rifts dotted the skyline like wounds in reality, and the glow of the Nexus towers had dimmed, casting long shadows over the city.

"We're too late," Lady Taryn said, her voice tight with urgency as she surveyed the landscape. "The rifts are spreading faster than we thought."

Vivian's heart raced as he took in the scene before them. The city, once a beacon of impossible science and magic, was now teetering on the edge of destruction. Everywhere he looked, reality was unraveling—buildings flickered in and out of existence, streets twisted in impossible ways, and people were trapped in loops, their movements distorted by time fractures.

Professor Arcturus, his face pale with concern, stepped forward. "We need to get to the Nexus core. If the central stabilizer is still intact, we might be able to stop the rifts from spreading further."

"But the figure..." Vivian began, his mind still spinning from their encounter in his home world. "They said this was just the beginning. If they've already unleashed the Elders' power—"

"Then we don't have much time," the professor finished grimly. "If the Elders are involved, the Nexus is more vulnerable than ever. We need to act quickly."

The trio made their way through the twisting streets, moving as fast as the shifting landscape would allow. As they passed through the heart of the city, Vivian saw Guardians of the Nexus fighting back against the chaos—wielding weapons of light and energy, they struck at the tendrils of dark force that erupted from the rifts, trying to contain the damage.

But it was clear that the Guardians were losing ground.

Towers that had stood for centuries began to crumble, their foundations weakened by the instability spreading through the city. The streets buckled and split, and rifts opened in the sky, raining down shards of distorted reality. The chaos was no longer confined to the edges of the multiverse—it was tearing through the very heart of the Nexus.

"We're running out of time," Lady Taryn said, her expression grim as they neared the central tower of the Nexus, where the core—the stabilizing force of the entire multiverse—was housed. "If the core fails, the entire multiverse will collapse into chaos."

Vivian felt a surge of fear. The idea that everything—the countless worlds, dimensions, lives—could simply unravel was almost too much to bear. But he knew they had to keep going. He had come too far, learned too much, to let it all end like this.

As they approached the tower, the ground shook violently, and a massive rift tore through the air in front of them. From within the rift, dark, swirling figures emerged—chaotic beings, twisted and fragmented, their forms barely holding together as they drifted toward the Nexus core.

"The Elders' servants," Professor Arcturus whispered, his face pale with recognition. "They've sent their creatures to finish what they started."

Lady Taryn drew her sword, its silver light flaring to life as she stepped forward. "I'll hold them off. Get to the core and stabilize it before it's too late."

"No," Vivian said, stepping up beside her, the Quantum Spark glowing faintly in his hand. "You won't fight them alone. We'll do this together."

Lady Taryn glanced at him, her expression softening for just a moment. "You've grown strong, Vivian. But be careful. These creatures feed on chaos—they're not bound by the rules of this reality."

Vivian nodded, his heart pounding as the first of the chaotic beings drifted toward them. He could feel the weight of their presence—like a black hole, pulling at the edges of reality, warping time and space around them.

Without hesitation, Lady Taryn launched herself into the fray, her sword cutting through the air with a flash of silver light. The creatures hissed and recoiled, but they were relentless, their dark tendrils lashing out toward her.

Vivian raised the Quantum Spark, feeling its energy surge through him. He focused on the rifts, sending threads of light toward them, trying to weave the fabric of reality back together before more creatures could emerge. The effort was exhausting—each rift seemed to resist him, fighting back as the chaotic energy tried to break free.

One of the creatures lunged toward him, its form twisting and distorting as it moved. Vivian barely had time to react, raising the Quantum Spark to form a barrier just before the creature struck. The impact sent a shockwave of energy through him, but the barrier held.

Beside him, Professor Arcturus was using his own magic, summoning glowing runes to form a protective circle around them. The creatures screeched and writhed as they struck the barrier, their forms flickering as they tried to break through.

"We can't keep this up forever," the professor said, his voice strained with effort. "We need to get to the core now."

Vivian nodded, his mind racing. The core—the stabilizing force of the entire Nexus—was their only hope. If they could reach it and use the Quantum Spark to reinforce its energy, they might be able to push back the chaos long enough to stop the rifts from spreading.

But the creatures were everywhere, and the rifts were multiplying. Every second they spent fighting was another second closer to total collapse.

"I'll clear a path," Vivian said, his voice steady despite the chaos swirling around them. He focused all his energy on the Quantum Spark, feeling its power surge through him.

With a shout, he unleashed a wave of energy, sending tendrils of light arcing through the air. The creatures hissed and recoiled as the light struck them, dissolving their forms into mist. The rifts flickered, their edges pulling back as the fabric of reality fought to reassert itself.

"Go!" Lady Taryn shouted, slashing through another creature as it lunged toward her. "I'll hold them here. Get to the core!"

Vivian exchanged a glance with the professor, who nodded grimly. Together, they ran toward the central tower, their footsteps echoing through the crumbling streets.

As they approached the entrance to the tower, the ground shook violently, and a deafening roar filled the air. The rifts above them expanded, and the sky itself seemed to tear apart, revealing a swirling void of darkness beyond.

The professor's face was pale with fear. "If we don't stop this now, the Nexus will fall. We're running out of time."

Vivian's heart pounded in his chest as they entered the tower, the heavy doors slamming shut behind them. Inside, the air was thick with tension, and the walls seemed to pulse with the energy of the Nexus core.

At the center of the room stood the core itself—a massive, glowing sphere of light, its surface crackling with energy. But even the core was flickering, its light dimming as the chaos spread through the Nexus.

"We need to stabilize it," Professor Arcturus said, his voice urgent. "The Quantum Spark should be able to reinforce the core's energy, but you'll need to connect with it directly."

Vivian nodded, stepping forward. He could feel the immense power radiating from the core, but it was unstable—fractured, like a dying star. The rifts had weakened it, and if they didn't act fast, the core would collapse, taking the entire multiverse with it.

Taking a deep breath, Vivian raised the Quantum Spark, its light flaring as he reached out with his mind. He could feel the connection forming, the energy of the core reaching toward the Spark, trying to stabilize itself.

But something was wrong.

As soon as Vivian made contact, a dark presence surged through the connection. It was the figure—the same being who had unleashed the chaos. Their power was still here, buried deep within the core, like a virus eating away at the Nexus from the inside.

"You cannot stop what has already begun," the figure's voice echoed in his mind. "The multiverse will fall, and from its ashes, chaos will reign."

Vivian gritted his teeth, pushing back against the presence. He could feel the weight of the figure's power pressing down on him, trying to overwhelm him. But he couldn't give in—not now.

"Vivian!" the professor called, his voice tense. "You have to sever the connection!"

Vivian's heart raced. He knew what needed to be done—but severing the connection meant cutting off the figure's influence over the Nexus. It also meant risking his own connection to the Quantum Spark. If he failed, the rifts would consume everything.

Taking a deep breath, Vivian focused all his energy on the Spark, feeling its power flow through him. He could sense the threads of the figure's influence woven deep within the core, corrupting its energy. Slowly, carefully, he began to unravel those threads, pulling them free from the core's light.

The presence fought back, lashing out with waves of chaotic energy, but Vivian held firm. He could feel the strain of the effort, but he refused to let go.

With a final surge of power, he severed the connection.

The dark presence let out a furious scream, and for a moment, the entire room trembled as the figure's influence was ripped away from the core. The rifts flickered violently, but then, slowly, they began to close.

The core's light flared brightly, its energy stabilizing as the rifts sealed themselves shut. The Nexus was holding—barely, but it was holding.

Vivian staggered back, his body trembling with exhaustion. He had done it. They had stopped the figure—for now.

But the battle was far from over.

Professor Arcturus rushed to his side, helping him stand. "You did it," he said, his voice filled with relief. "The Nexus is stable, but we still have a long fight ahead of us."

Vivian nodded, his mind spinning with the weight of what had just happened. The figure's presence was gone from the Nexus core, but the rifts had already spread to other dimensions. The chaos was still out there, waiting for its next opportunity.

As they stood together in the flickering light of the Nexus core, Vivian knew that the true battle was yet to come.

The figure had been right about one thing: chaos couldn't be contained forever.

But as long as he had the Quantum Spark, and the strength to wield it, Vivian would fight to protect the multiverse—and the Nexus that held it together.

Chapter 16: The Eye of the Storm

The Nexus, though temporarily stabilized, was not the same. The shimmering towers and floating platforms were dimmer, the once vibrant streets quieter as the citizens of the city attempted to recover from the chaos that had ravaged their home. The core had been saved, but the echoes of the battle still resonated in the air—a reminder that the worst was yet to come.

Vivian sat at the edge of a platform overlooking the city, his gaze drifting across the fractured skyline. His mind was buzzing, the weight of everything that had happened pressing down on him. He had saved the Nexus, but the rifts were still out there—spreading through the multiverse, threatening to tear apart reality itself.

And the figure—the one who had caused all of this—was still out there, waiting for the right moment to strike again.

"You did well back there," Professor Arcturus said as he approached, his voice gentle. He sat beside Vivian, his expression weary but proud. "The Nexus owes you its survival."

Vivian shook his head. "It's not over, though. We just bought ourselves time. The figure—whoever they are—they're still out there. They're not going to stop until the Nexus falls."

The professor nodded, his gaze distant. "You're right. But now we have a chance to stop them. The Nexus core is stable for the moment, but the rifts are still spreading. We need to find the source, the heart of the chaos, and stop it once and for all."

Vivian's heart clenched as he thought about the figure's words, the promise that chaos couldn't be contained forever. He had seen what unchecked power could do—how it could warp reality, break time, and destroy entire worlds. And now, more than ever, he felt the burden of the Quantum Spark, the artifact that had connected him to this vast and fragile multiverse.

"What if I'm not strong enough?" Vivian asked quietly, his eyes fixed on the swirling clouds above. "What if I can't stop them?"

Professor Arcturus turned to him, his voice steady but filled with understanding. "The strength of the Quantum Spark is not just in its power, but in the one who wields it. You've already proven that you have the ability to shape reality, to control the chaos. But more than that, you have the heart to use that power wisely. That's what sets you apart from the figure. They want to control the multiverse for themselves. You want to protect it."

Vivian nodded slowly, though doubt still lingered in the back of his mind. He had seen what power could do—how it could corrupt, twist even the most well-meaning intentions. And deep down, he feared that if he wasn't careful, he might fall down the same path as the figure.

"We're not alone in this fight," Professor Arcturus said after a long moment. "The Guardians are preparing for battle. Lady Taryn has called for reinforcements from the outer dimensions. And there are others who will stand with us—people who understand the importance of balance and who will fight to protect it."

Vivian took a deep breath, the weight of responsibility still heavy on his shoulders but softened by the professor's words. He wasn't alone. He had allies—people who believed in the same things he did. And together, they could stop the figure from tearing the multiverse apart.

But just as he was beginning to gather his resolve, something strange happened.

The air around them shifted, growing colder, and the faint hum of the Nexus seemed to fade, replaced by a low, resonant vibration. It was a sound that Vivian recognized immediately—a sound that signaled the presence of a rift.

Professor Arcturus stood up sharply, his eyes narrowing as he scanned the horizon. "Another rift. But this one feels... different."

Vivian felt it too. The rift wasn't like the others they had encountered. This one carried a deeper, more intense energy—like a storm building in the distance, ready to unleash its fury. The sky above them darkened further, and the familiar flickering of reality signaled that something—or someone—was coming.

And then, the rift appeared.

It tore through the sky with a deafening crack, a jagged line of darkness that pulsed with chaotic energy. But instead of spilling fragmented time and space like the other rifts, this one remained steady, its form held together by an unseen force.

From within the rift, a figure emerged.

It was the same cloaked figure that had haunted their journey, the one who had caused the chaos to spread across the multiverse. But now, the figure's presence was even more imposing, their aura radiating raw, unchecked power. The air around them shimmered with dark energy, and the rift behind them pulsed like a heartbeat.

"So, we meet again," the figure said, their voice smooth but filled with menace. "I've been waiting for this moment."

Professor Arcturus stepped forward, his hand raised as he summoned glowing runes into the air, preparing to defend against the attack he knew was coming. "You've caused enough damage. The Nexus won't fall to your chaos."

The figure tilted their head slightly, as though considering the professor's words. "Damage? No. This is not damage. This is evolution. The multiverse was never meant to be bound by rules, by balance. Chaos is the natural state of all things, and I will see it restored."

"You're wrong," Vivian said, stepping up beside the professor, his voice steady despite the fear twisting inside him. "Chaos like this will destroy everything. The Nexus was built to protect the multiverse—to keep it from collapsing into chaos. Without it, there's nothing but destruction."

The figure let out a low chuckle, the sound dark and cold. "You still don't understand, do you? The Nexus is a prison. It was built to contain the infinite potential of the multiverse, to keep it shackled by rules and laws that were never meant to exist. I am simply breaking those chains—releasing the true power of the multiverse."

Vivian's heart pounded as the figure's words sank in. There was something almost hypnotic about the way they spoke—something that pulled at the edges of his mind, making him question everything he had believed about the Nexus, about balance, about chaos.

But then, through the haze of doubt, he heard the professor's voice.

"Don't listen to them, Vivian. They're trying to manipulate you—trying to twist the truth. The Nexus isn't a prison. It's a safeguard. Without it, the multiverse would unravel. We've already seen what happens when the rifts spread."

Vivian took a deep breath, grounding himself in the professor's words. He knew what he had seen—he had seen the destruction that chaos could cause, the lives shattered by rifts that tore apart time and space. He couldn't let the figure continue to spread their influence, no matter how convincing their arguments seemed.

"You're wrong," Vivian said again, his voice stronger this time. "Chaos might be a part of the multiverse, but it's not everything. There has to be balance. Without it, everything falls apart."

The figure's glowing eyes narrowed beneath their hood. "You've grown strong, apprentice. Stronger than I anticipated. But strength alone won't save you."

With a sudden motion, the figure raised their hand, and the rift behind them flared with energy. Dark tendrils of chaotic force shot toward Vivian and the professor, crackling with destructive power.

Professor Arcturus reacted quickly, summoning a barrier of light to block the attack. The tendrils slammed into the barrier, sending shockwaves of energy through the air, but the barrier held—for now.

"You have no idea what you're dealing with," the figure said, their voice cold and sharp. "The power of the Elders runs through me. You cannot stop what has already begun."

Vivian's heart raced as he raised the Quantum Spark, feeling its energy surge through him. He knew the figure was powerful—perhaps more powerful than anyone he had faced before—but he also knew that they couldn't let the figure win. If they lost here, the Nexus—and the entire multiverse—would fall.

The figure unleashed another wave of chaotic energy, and this time, the barrier cracked under the pressure. The professor's face was strained with effort as he struggled to maintain the shield.

"Vivian, now!" the professor shouted. "You have to sever their connection to the rift!"

Vivian nodded, focusing all his energy on the Quantum Spark. He could feel the pull of the rift—the dark, swirling power that connected the figure to the chaos spreading through the multiverse. He had to break that connection, or the figure would overwhelm them.

With a deep breath, he raised the Spark, sending threads of light toward the rift. The energy crackled in the air as it reached the edges of the tear in reality, trying to close it.

But the figure wasn't finished.

"You think you can stop me?" they hissed, their voice filled with fury. "I am beyond the Nexus. I am beyond balance. I am chaos itself!"

The rift flared with energy, and for a moment, Vivian felt the overwhelming weight of the figure's power pressing down on him. The darkness surged, trying to break through his defenses, to pull him into the chaos.

But then, through the storm of power, Vivian felt something else—a presence, a strength that came not from the Quantum Spark, but from within himself. It was the same strength he had felt when he first connected with the Spark, the same force that had driven him to protect the multiverse.

He wasn't just fighting to stop the figure. He was fighting for the people he had met, the worlds he had seen, the balance that held the multiverse together.

And with that realization, the fear that had gripped him faded.

Vivian reached deeper into the Spark's power, feeling it respond to his will. The threads of light grew brighter, pushing back against the rift's chaotic energy. Slowly, the tear in reality began to close, the darkness pulling inward as the fabric of the multiverse knitted itself back together.

The figure let out a furious scream as the rift shrank, their form flickering as the connection between them and the chaos weakened.

"You cannot stop me!" the figure shouted, their voice echoing with rage. "The multiverse will fall! Chaos will reign!"

Vivian gritted his teeth, pushing harder, his mind focused entirely on sealing the rift. The figure's power was immense, but he could feel their influence slipping away. Slowly, inch by inch, the rift closed, the darkness retreating as the light of the Quantum Spark filled the space.

And then, with a final surge of energy, the rift snapped shut.

The figure staggered back, their form flickering in and out of existence as the last traces of chaotic energy faded. For a moment, they stood there, their glowing eyes fixed on Vivian.

"You've delayed the inevitable," they whispered, their voice hollow. "But chaos cannot be contained forever."

With a final, flickering movement, the figure dissolved into the air, leaving only silence in their wake.

For a long moment, Vivian stood still, his body trembling with exhaustion but his mind sharp and clear. The rift was gone, the figure defeated—for now.

Professor Arcturus placed a hand on his shoulder, his voice filled with pride. "You did it, Vivian. You severed their connection to the chaos."

Vivian nodded, though he knew that the battle was far from over. The figure might have been defeated, but the chaos they had unleashed was still out there, waiting for its next opportunity to strike.

As they stood together, the air around them calm but charged with the tension of what was to come, Vivian felt a sense of resolve settle over him.

The eye of the storm had passed—but the true battle was still on the horizon.

Chapter 17: The Final Convergence

The calm that had settled over the Nexus in the aftermath of the battle with the figure was a fleeting illusion. Even as the city stood momentarily stable, rifts continued to flicker at the edges of reality, and the pulse of chaos could still be felt, a constant reminder that the true storm had not yet passed.

Vivian stood at the heart of the Nexus core chamber, his hand resting lightly on the surface of the glowing sphere. It pulsed steadily now, the light stronger, but he knew that it was a fragile stability. The core had been saved from immediate collapse, but the chaos was still out there, threatening to tear apart the multiverse one rift at a time.

Professor Arcturus stood beside him, his expression tense as he studied the holographic display in front of them. The map of the multiverse showed the spread of the rifts—like cracks in a mirror, branching outward from the Nexus and touching countless dimensions.

"We've stabilized the core for now," the professor said quietly, "but the rifts are still expanding. Whatever the figure is planning, they're not finished. They're still out there, and the chaos is growing stronger."

Vivian nodded, his mind racing. He could still feel the weight of the figure's presence—the cold, dark power that had nearly overwhelmed him during their last encounter. They had severed the figure's connection to the rifts in the Nexus, but it was only a temporary victory. The figure had retreated, but they weren't defeated.

"Do we know where the next attack will be?" Vivian asked, his voice steady despite the tension he felt.

Professor Arcturus gestured to the map, where several key dimensions were highlighted. "The figure has been focusing their efforts on the outer dimensions—the places where the fabric of reality is weakest. If they can destabilize those dimensions, it will cause a ripple effect, eventually tearing through the core dimensions, including the Nexus itself."

Vivian's heart sank as he studied the map. The outer dimensions were fragile, often overlooked in the grand scheme of the multiverse. They weren't as stable as the central worlds, and if the figure succeeded in unraveling them, the chaos would spread uncontrollably.

"We need to stop them before they can tear through the outer dimensions," Vivian said, determination hardening in his voice. "If we can find where they're hiding, we can stop this before it gets worse."

"We have an idea," came a voice from the doorway.

Lady Taryn entered the chamber, her silver armor gleaming in the light of the core. Behind her, several Guardians of the Nexus stood at attention, their faces grim with the weight of the coming battle.

"We've detected a massive surge of chaotic energy in one of the outer dimensions," Lady Taryn continued. "The energy signature matches the figure's presence. We believe they've gathered their forces for a final attack."

Vivian's pulse quickened. "Which dimension?"

Lady Taryn stepped forward, activating the map. One of the highlighted dimensions pulsed with dark energy—a world on the farthest edge of the multiverse, one that Vivian had never visited before.

"Dimension Theta-9," she said. "It's a small world, but it's uniquely positioned at the convergence of several dimensional currents. If the figure destabilizes it, the energy will ripple through the multiverse, causing rifts to form in every dimension simultaneously."

"That's where they'll make their final stand," Professor Arcturus said, his expression grave. "If they succeed, the multiverse will collapse."

Vivian took a deep breath, his heart racing as the full scope of the figure's plan came into focus. This was the moment they had been preparing for—the final convergence, where the forces of chaos would either be stopped or unleashed in full.

"We need to move now," Lady Taryn said, her voice firm. "The Guardians are ready to launch an assault on Dimension Theta-9. But we'll need you, Vivian. The figure's connection to the chaos is too strong for us to sever without the Quantum Spark."

Vivian nodded, feeling the weight of the Spark pulsing in his hand. The battle ahead would be the hardest he had ever faced, but he knew that the fate of the multiverse rested on their success.

"We'll go," Vivian said, his voice steady. "We'll stop them, once and for all."

The journey to Dimension Theta-9 was swift, but the sense of impending doom weighed heavily on the group as they stepped through the shimmering portal. The moment they arrived, Vivian could feel it—an overwhelming presence of chaotic energy that filled the air, warping time and space around them.

The world itself was bleak, a vast expanse of dark rock and swirling clouds that stretched out into infinity. In the distance, a massive rift loomed, larger than any they had seen before, its edges crackling with dark energy. And at the center of it all stood the figure.

They were waiting for them.

Vivian, Lady Taryn, Professor Arcturus, and the Guardians of the Nexus spread out, preparing for the battle ahead. The tension in the air was palpable, and the ground beneath them trembled as the figure's power rippled through the dimension.

"You've come, as I knew you would," the figure said, their voice echoing across the desolate landscape. "But you're too late. The rift is already opening. Soon, the chaos will spread, and the multiverse will be free from its chains."

Vivian stepped forward, the Quantum Spark glowing brightly in his hand. "This isn't freedom," he said, his voice firm. "You're not saving the multiverse—you're destroying it."

The figure tilted their head slightly, as though considering his words. "You still don't understand. The multiverse was never meant to be bound by balance, by rules. Chaos is the natural state of all things. I am simply returning the multiverse to what it was always meant to be—unlimited, unbound, free."

"Chaos isn't freedom," Professor Arcturus said, his voice sharp. "It's destruction. Without balance, the multiverse would tear itself apart."

The figure's eyes glowed with dark energy. "You speak of balance as though it's some sacred thing, but it's nothing more than a cage. A cage that you've built to keep the multiverse from reaching its true potential. But that cage is about to shatter."

With a wave of their hand, the figure unleashed a torrent of chaotic energy, sending shockwaves through the dimension. The ground cracked and split beneath them, and the rift behind the figure began to pulse with dark energy, growing larger with each passing moment.

"Guardians, now!" Lady Taryn shouted, raising her sword as the Guardians surged forward, their weapons glowing with light.

The battle erupted in a flash of energy, the Guardians clashing with the figure's chaotic forces. Tendrils of dark energy lashed out from the rift, striking at the Guardians as they fought to push back the chaos.

Vivian focused all his energy on the Quantum Spark, sending threads of light toward the rift, trying to stabilize it before it could grow any larger. But the figure's power was overwhelming, and every time Vivian tried to close the rift, the figure countered, sending waves of chaotic force crashing against his defenses.

"You cannot stop me, apprentice," the figure hissed, their voice filled with fury. "The Elders have already awakened. Their power flows through the rift, and soon, it will consume everything."

Vivian gritted his teeth, pushing back with all his strength. The weight of the figure's power pressed down on him, but he refused to give in. He could feel the energy of the Spark growing stronger, pulsing in rhythm with the multiverse itself.

"You're wrong," Vivian said, his voice steady despite the chaos swirling around him. "There's more to the multiverse than chaos.

There's life, there's creation, there's balance. And I won't let you take that away."

With a surge of energy, Vivian unleashed a wave of light from the Quantum Spark, sending it crashing toward the rift. The light struck the edges of the rift, and for a moment, the chaotic energy recoiled.

But the figure wasn't finished.

"You think you can stop me?" they shouted, their voice filled with rage. "You're nothing more than a child playing with power you don't understand!"

The figure raised their hands, and the rift exploded with dark energy. The sky above them ripped open, revealing the swirling chaos of the multiverse beyond. The ground beneath them shook violently, and Vivian felt a wave of fear surge through him.

But then, through the storm of chaos, he heard the professor's voice.

"Vivian, focus! You have the power to stop this!"

Vivian's heart pounded as he looked up at the rift, the dark energy swirling around it like a storm. He could feel the figure's power, the overwhelming presence of the Elders, pressing down on him, trying to break him.

But he wasn't alone.

Lady Taryn and the Guardians fought valiantly against the figure's forces, their light cutting through the darkness. And Professor Arcturus stood beside him, his eyes filled with confidence and trust.

Vivian took a deep breath, his mind clearing as he connected with the Quantum Spark. He could feel the threads of the multiverse around him, the delicate balance that held everything together. The figure was trying to unravel that balance, to release the chaos that lay beneath the surface.

But Vivian had the power to stop it.

With a shout, Vivian raised the Quantum Spark, sending a surge of energy toward the rift. The light spread through the air like a web, reaching out to the edges of the tear in reality. Slowly, the rift began to shrink, the chaotic energy pulling inward as the light of the Spark filled the space.

The figure let out a furious scream as their connection to the rift weakened. "No! This cannot be!"

But Vivian didn't stop. He focused all his energy on the Spark, feeling its power surge through him. He could feel the multiverse responding, the threads of reality knitting themselves back together as the rift shrank further.

With one final surge of power, the rift snapped shut.

The figure staggered back, their form flickering as the last traces of chaotic energy faded. For a moment, they stood there, their glowing eyes fixed on Vivian.

"You think you've won," they whispered, their voice hollow. "But chaos cannot be contained. It will return. And when it does, you will fall."

And with that, the figure dissolved into the air, disappearing into the shadows.

For a long moment, the world was silent. The rift was gone, and the chaotic energy that had threatened to tear the multiverse apart had faded. The battle was over.

Vivian collapsed to the ground, his body trembling with exhaustion but his heart filled with relief. They had done it. They had stopped the figure, and the multiverse had been saved—at least for now.

Professor Arcturus knelt beside him, a proud smile on his face. "You did it, Vivian. You stopped them."

Vivian nodded, though he knew that the figure's words still hung over them like a shadow. The chaos might have been contained, but the figure was right about one thing: chaos could never be truly defeated.

As they stood together, the dark clouds above them began to clear, revealing the infinite stars of the multiverse beyond. The Nexus had been saved, and the balance had been restored.

But as Vivian looked out over the horizon, he knew that the battle for the multiverse was far from over.

There would always be forces that sought to disrupt the balance, to unleash chaos on a fragile reality. And as long as the Quantum Spark remained in his hand, Vivian would stand ready to protect the multiverse from whatever came next.

Chapter 18: The Aftermath of Chaos

The battle was over. The chaotic rift had been sealed, and the figure's shadowy presence had finally faded. But the sense of victory felt bittersweet.

Vivian stood on the cracked surface of Dimension Theta-9, the once chaotic energies that had filled the air now settling into an eerie stillness. All around him, the Guardians were tending to the wounded and surveying the damage. Lady Taryn was issuing orders, her silver armor stained with the marks of battle, but her voice calm and steady.

Professor Arcturus approached him, his face lined with exhaustion but relief shining in his eyes. "It's over," he said softly, placing a hand on Vivian's shoulder. "You did it."

Vivian nodded, though his mind felt clouded. The adrenaline from the battle had left him, and now the weight of everything that had happened pressed down on him like a heavy cloak. He had saved the multiverse, but at what cost?

He glanced down at the Quantum Spark, still glowing faintly in his hand. It was a reminder of the power he wielded—and the responsibility that came with it. In the silence after the battle, he couldn't shake the figure's final words from his mind: *Chaos will return. And when it does, you will fall.*

"I just... I don't feel like it's really over," Vivian said quietly, staring out at the distant horizon of the shattered dimension. "They might be gone, but what's stopping chaos from coming back? What if it happens again?"

Professor Arcturus sighed, his expression thoughtful. "Chaos is part of the multiverse, just as order is. There will always be forces that seek to disrupt the balance. But you've proven today that it can be fought, that it can be contained. And more than that, you've proven that the Nexus—and the multiverse—has protectors."

Vivian wasn't sure if that was entirely reassuring, but he knew the professor was right. The multiverse was vast and unpredictable, and there would always be new challenges. But that didn't mean they were helpless. The Guardians, the Nexus, and the Quantum Spark were all part of that delicate balance.

As the rift in Dimension Theta-9 finally faded into nothingness, leaving behind a fragile but stable world, Lady Taryn approached, her face set in a firm but proud expression.

"The rifts are closing," she said, her voice calm despite the exhaustion in her eyes. "Thanks to you, Vivian. The damage the figure caused was significant, but we've stabilized the outer dimensions. The Nexus will recover."

Vivian felt a flicker of relief. Knowing that the damage was repairable made the weight on his shoulders feel a little lighter. "What about the figure?" he asked. "Are they really gone?"

Lady Taryn's gaze hardened. "They may be defeated, but they're not gone. The forces they awakened are ancient, powerful, and they've likely retreated to the dark spaces between dimensions. For now, the immediate threat has passed, but we must remain vigilant."

Professor Arcturus nodded in agreement. "The figure is a servant of chaos, and chaos never fully disappears. But you've made sure it won't reign unchecked—not today, and not for a long time."

Vivian took a deep breath, the enormity of it all finally settling in. The multiverse had been on the brink of destruction, and they had pulled it back from the edge. But the battle had changed him in ways he couldn't yet fully grasp. He felt older, wiser, and perhaps a little more wary of the power he wielded.

The Guardians were beginning to gather, preparing to return to the Nexus and leave the devastated dimension behind. Lady Taryn offered Vivian a small, respectful nod. "You fought well today, Vivian. The Nexus owes you its survival. But know this: the Quantum Spark is not just a weapon or a tool. It's a responsibility. And the choice of how to use it will always be yours."

Vivian nodded, understanding her words. The Quantum Spark had given him incredible power, but it had also tested him in ways he hadn't anticipated. He had faced the lure of chaos, the temptation to wield that power recklessly, and he had chosen to stand for balance. But he knew that choice would need to be made again, time and time again.

"Thank you, Lady Taryn," he said, his voice quiet but steady. "I'll do everything I can to protect the balance."

With that, the Guardians activated the portal, and one by one, they began to step through, returning to the Nexus. Vivian, Professor Arcturus, and Lady Taryn were the last to leave the dimension, the once chaotic landscape now eerily quiet as the portal closed behind them.

Back in the Nexus, the city was slowly coming back to life. The towers, once flickering and unstable, now glowed with a steady light, and the streets, though still marked by the signs of battle, were filled with people working to rebuild. Vivian felt a sense of pride as he walked through the city—this place, this impossible fusion of science and magic, had survived the storm.

But even as the city recovered, Vivian knew that the damage ran deeper than the physical scars. The multiverse itself had been shaken by the chaos, and the echoes of the figure's influence would be felt for a long time to come.

Professor Arcturus and Vivian made their way back to the Institute, where a small group of scholars and scientists were already working to study the effects of the rifts and the chaos that had spread through the multiverse. They were collecting data, analyzing the patterns, trying to understand how to prevent something like this from happening again.

Vivian watched them for a moment, his mind still buzzing with everything that had happened. The world had changed—he had changed. And he wasn't sure what the future held.

As they reached the professor's study, Arcturus turned to him, his expression serious but warm. "You've come a long way, Vivian. From the moment you first arrived here, I knew you were destined for something important. But I couldn't have imagined just how important."

Vivian smiled faintly, though he still felt the weight of his responsibilities. "I never thought I'd end up here," he admitted. "Back home, everything felt so... ordinary. I didn't know there was something more out there. But now I see that the multiverse is bigger and more complicated than I could have ever imagined."

The professor nodded. "That's the nature of the multiverse. It's always changing, always revealing new mysteries. And you've only just begun to understand it. But I believe you're ready for whatever comes next."

Vivian looked down at the Quantum Spark, still glowing faintly in his hand. It felt both familiar and foreign at the same time—a reminder of the power he held, but also the responsibility that came with it. He wasn't the same person who had first volunteered to test the time machine all those months ago. He had seen things, faced things, that had changed him forever.

"What do we do now?" Vivian asked, his voice thoughtful.

"We rebuild," Professor Arcturus said simply. "We learn from what happened, and we prepare for the future. The figure may be gone for now, but chaos will always be part of the multiverse. Our job is to protect the balance, to ensure that the rifts don't spiral out of control again."

Vivian nodded, feeling a sense of resolution settle over him. The battle might be over, but the journey was far from finished. He had a new purpose now, a new understanding of the multiverse and his place within it.

As they stood together in the quiet study, the light of the Nexus glowing softly through the windows, Vivian felt something he hadn't expected—hope. Hope for the future, for the people of the Nexus, and for the endless possibilities that lay ahead.

Whatever challenges came next, whatever chaos threatened to rise again, he knew he wasn't alone. He had the professor, the Guardians, and the Quantum Spark.

And as long as he had the strength to protect the balance, the multiverse would endure.

Chapter 19: A New Dawn

The days that followed the final battle were filled with a quiet sense of recovery. As the Nexus began to heal, so too did the people within it. The shimmering towers, once flickering with instability, now stood tall and proud, their light casting a warm glow over the city. The air, once charged with tension and fear, felt lighter. Yet, there was a solemnity that remained—a shared understanding of how close they had come to losing everything.

Vivian wandered the streets of the Nexus, watching as scholars, scientists, and engineers worked side by side to repair the damage caused by the chaos. Guardians stood watch at the city's edges, ensuring that any lingering rifts were closed before they could spread. The Nexus was alive with purpose, and for the first time since the battle, Vivian felt a sense of calm.

His thoughts, however, were still racing. The figure's final words echoed in his mind, a constant reminder that chaos was never truly gone. But rather than fear, those words filled Vivian with a deeper resolve. He knew now that his journey wasn't over—not by a long shot.

As he reached the central square of the Nexus, he saw Professor Arcturus speaking with Lady Taryn and a group of Guardians. Their conversation was serious, but there was a quiet optimism in their expressions. The Nexus had survived the storm, and now they were preparing for whatever came next.

Lady Taryn spotted Vivian and approached, her silver armor gleaming in the light. She offered him a small smile, her eyes filled with respect.

"You've done well, Vivian," she said, her voice strong but warm. "The Nexus wouldn't be standing if it weren't for you."

Vivian shifted slightly, feeling both pride and humility. "I didn't do it alone," he replied. "We all fought for the Nexus. And I know we'll have to fight again someday."

Lady Taryn nodded. "Chaos will always be a part of the multiverse. But so will those who stand for balance. You've proven that the Spark chose its wielder wisely."

Vivian glanced down at the Quantum Spark, which now rested comfortably in his hand. It felt like a part of him—an extension of who he was. But more than that, it represented the choice he had made to protect the multiverse and its infinite possibilities.

"Thank you," Vivian said, his voice filled with sincerity. "For everything."

Lady Taryn gave a respectful nod before returning to the Guardians. Vivian watched them for a moment, feeling a sense of camaraderie with the people who had fought beside him. The Nexus was more than just a city—it was a symbol of hope and resilience, a place where science and magic met to create something extraordinary.

As he turned to continue his walk, he felt a familiar presence beside him.

Professor Arcturus had finished his conversation with the Guardians and now stood by Vivian's side, his expression soft but thoughtful.

"How are you feeling?" the professor asked, his voice gentle.

Vivian smiled faintly, though there was a touch of uncertainty in his eyes. "I don't know, honestly. I'm proud of what we did, but I also know that this isn't the end. The multiverse is always changing, and chaos is always out there, waiting for the right moment."

The professor nodded, his eyes filled with understanding. "You're right. The work of protecting the multiverse is never truly finished. There will always be new challenges, new threats. But you've proven that you're more than capable of handling whatever comes your way."

Vivian's smile grew a little wider. "I guess I'm still trying to wrap my head around everything. Not too long ago, I was just a kid who thought school was boring and that life didn't have anything exciting to offer. Now... everything's different."

Professor Arcturus chuckled softly. "Life has a way of surprising us, doesn't it? But that's the beauty of the multiverse. It's full of possibilities—some we can't even begin to imagine."

Vivian nodded, his heart lightening as he thought about the future. There was so much left to explore, so much to learn. The multiverse was vast, and he had only scratched the surface of what it had to offer.

As they walked together through the heart of the Nexus, the city bustling with life around them, Vivian realized that he had found something he hadn't even known he was looking for—purpose. The adventures, the battles, the challenges he had faced—all of it had led him to this moment, where he finally understood his place in the multiverse.

"I've been thinking," Vivian said after a moment of silence. "About what comes next."

Professor Arcturus raised an eyebrow, intrigued. "Oh?"

"Yeah," Vivian continued. "I don't want to just wait for the next crisis. I want to be ready. I want to learn more about the multiverse, about the different dimensions, the way everything is connected. I feel like there's so much more out there that I don't understand yet."

The professor smiled, his eyes filled with pride. "That's a wise approach. The more we understand the multiverse, the better prepared we are to protect it. And you, my boy, have a gift for seeing beyond what most people notice. You've always had that curiosity—the desire to know more, to explore the unknown."

Vivian grinned, feeling a spark of excitement return to him. "So... what do you say? Will you keep teaching me?"

Professor Arcturus laughed, his voice filled with warmth. "I would be honored to continue your education, Vivian. There's so much more to discover, and I can't think of anyone better suited for the task."

They continued walking, the Nexus glowing brightly in the soft light of the day. People passed by them, busy with their work, but Vivian felt a deep connection to each and every one of them. They were all part of something bigger—something extraordinary. And he was proud to be a part of it.

As they approached the entrance to the Nexus Institute, Vivian paused, turning to look back at the city behind him. It was strange to think about how much had changed since he first arrived here, unsure of what lay ahead. Now, he felt confident, grounded, and ready for whatever came next.

The future was uncertain—chaos was always waiting at the edges of the multiverse, and new challenges would arise. But Vivian knew that as long as he had the Quantum Spark, as long as he had the people of the Nexus by his side, they would face whatever came their way.

"Ready for the next adventure?" Professor Arcturus asked, his eyes twinkling with anticipation.

Vivian smiled, the weight of his responsibilities no longer a burden, but a source of strength. "Always."

Together, they stepped into the Institute, ready to face the endless possibilities of the multiverse.

Chapter 20: The Unwritten Future

The Nexus shone brighter than it had in days. The shimmering towers, the floating platforms, and the bustling streets had returned to their vibrant, impossible state. Life was thriving again, and the weight of chaos had lifted—for now.

Vivian stood on one of the highest balconies of the Nexus Institute, overlooking the sprawling city below. The view was breathtaking, but it wasn't the beauty of the Nexus that filled his mind—it was the journey that had led him here. The battles he had fought, the choices he had made, and the knowledge he had gained about the multiverse had transformed him from a boy seeking escape into someone with a deep sense of responsibility.

He hadn't expected this. When he had first volunteered to test the time machine at school, he had wanted to get away from the monotony of his life, to find something exciting and different. And he had found it—but in ways he could never have imagined.

Now, as the sun began to set over the city, casting a golden glow over the buildings, Vivian felt at peace. The chaos had been contained, and for the first time in what felt like a long while, he could breathe without the weight of imminent danger pressing down on him.

The door behind him creaked open, and Professor Arcturus stepped onto the balcony, his familiar presence comforting. He stood beside Vivian, gazing out at the same view.

"It's beautiful, isn't it?" the professor said softly, his voice filled with pride.

Vivian nodded, a small smile playing on his lips. "It really is. Sometimes I forget how amazing this place is. But today, it feels... different. More real."

The professor chuckled. "That's because you've earned this moment. You've fought hard to protect the Nexus, and now you can truly appreciate what it stands for."

Vivian glanced at the professor, his expression thoughtful. "Do you think it's really over? The figure... the chaos... will it ever come back?"

The professor's eyes softened. "Chaos is a part of the multiverse, just as balance is. It will return someday, in one form or another. But what matters is that when it does, there will always be those who stand ready to protect the balance. You've proven yourself to be one of those people, Vivian. And as long as there are protectors like you, the multiverse will endure."

Vivian's heart swelled with a mix of pride and determination. He had come so far, and while the future remained uncertain, he knew he was ready for whatever came next.

"Do you ever wonder what's out there?" Vivian asked after a moment, gesturing toward the distant skyline, where the faint outlines of other dimensions could almost be felt beyond the horizon.

Professor Arcturus smiled. "Every day. The multiverse is infinite—full of worlds we've never seen, mysteries we've yet to solve. That's what makes it so extraordinary. There's always more to discover, more to learn."

Vivian's curiosity stirred at the thought. The figure had been a powerful adversary, but they were just one force in a much larger, more complex multiverse. There were countless dimensions, each with its own challenges, its own stories waiting to be told.

"I want to explore them," Vivian said, his voice filled with quiet conviction. "Not just to protect the Nexus, but to understand it all. The connections between worlds, the way everything fits together... there's so much I don't know."

The professor nodded, his eyes twinkling with approval. "That's the mark of a true seeker of knowledge—never being satisfied with what you already know. The Nexus will always need protectors, but it also needs explorers, people who are willing to venture into the unknown and bring back what they've learned."

Vivian smiled, feeling a sense of purpose settle over him. "Then I guess that's what I'll do. I'll explore. I'll learn. And I'll be ready for whatever comes next."

The professor placed a hand on Vivian's shoulder, his gaze filled with pride. "You've grown more than I ever could have imagined. The Quantum Spark chose you for a reason, and now I see that reason clearly. You're not just a protector, Vivian—you're a bridge between worlds, someone who can connect the multiverse in ways we've never seen before."

Vivian looked down at the Quantum Spark in his hand, its glow soft but steady. It was more than just a tool or a weapon—it was a symbol of everything he had learned, everything he had become. The power to shape reality, to protect the balance, and to explore the infinite possibilities of the multiverse was now his.

And he was ready to use it.

As the sun dipped below the horizon, casting long shadows over the city, Vivian and the professor stood together in silence, watching as the Nexus came alive with the soft glow of lights, its streets bustling with the energy of people rebuilding and looking forward.

For the first time in what felt like forever, the future felt open—like a book waiting to be written. Vivian knew that the challenges wouldn't stop, that chaos would always be out there, lurking at the edges of reality. But he also knew that he wasn't alone.

He had the Nexus. He had Professor Arcturus. He had the Guardians and the Quantum Spark.

And most importantly, he had the courage to face whatever came next.

Epilogue: Into the Unknown

A few weeks had passed since the final battle, and the Nexus had fully returned to its normal rhythm. The rifts had closed, and the city was thriving once again. People moved through the streets with a sense of hope, knowing that they had faced chaos and survived.

Vivian stood at the edge of one of the Nexus's portals, ready to embark on his next journey. The destination: an uncharted dimension, a place no one from the Nexus had visited before. It was a world on the farthest edge of the multiverse, where the boundaries of reality were thin and strange phenomena were rumored to occur.

Professor Arcturus stood beside him, offering his final instructions before the journey. "Remember, this isn't just about fighting chaos. It's about learning, about understanding the connections that hold the multiverse together. Keep your mind open, and trust in the Spark."

Vivian nodded, his heart racing with excitement. He had prepared for this moment, but now that it was here, the sense of adventure was almost overwhelming.

"I'll be back before you know it," he said with a grin, stepping closer to the portal.

The professor smiled, though there was a hint of pride in his eyes. "I have no doubt. Good luck, Vivian. The multiverse has much to show you."

Vivian took a deep breath, his hand tightening around the Quantum Spark. With one last glance at the professor and the Nexus behind him, he stepped through the portal.

The air shimmered, and for a brief moment, Vivian felt the familiar sensation of weightlessness as he crossed the threshold between worlds. The light faded, and then he was standing in a new place—a world unlike anything he had ever seen before.

The sky above him was a swirling mix of colors, the ground beneath his feet soft and pulsing with life. Strange structures loomed in the distance, their shapes constantly shifting, as if reality itself was in flux.

Vivian smiled, the thrill of the unknown filling him with excitement. This was just the beginning—there was so much more to discover, so many worlds to explore, and so many mysteries waiting to be uncovered.

With the Quantum Spark in his hand and the knowledge he had gained, Vivian took his first step into the unknown, ready for whatever adventures lay ahead.